MARRIAGE AT THE MANOR

MARRIAGE AT THE MANOR

Amanda Grange

Chivers Press • **Thorndike Press**
Bath, England **Waterville, Maine USA**

This Large Print edition is published by Chivers Press, England, and by Thorndike Press, USA.

Published in 2003 in the U.K. by arrangement with Robert Hale Ltd.

Published in 2003 in the U.S. by arrangement with Robert Hale Limited.

U.K. Hardcover   ISBN 0–7540–8986–X (Chivers Large Print)
U.K. Softcover   ISBN 0–7540–8987–8 (Camden Large Print)
U.S. Softcover   ISBN 0–7862–5419–X (General Series)

The text of this Large Print edition is unabridged.
Other aspects of the book may vary from the original edition.

Set in 16 pt. New Times Roman.

Printed in Great Britain on acid-free paper.

British Library Cataloguing in Publication Data available

ISBN 0–7862–5419–X (lg. print : sc : alk. paper)

For my uncle, Fred

CHAPTER ONE

'Are you sure?' asked Mr Weedon. 'It's still not too late to change your mind.'

Miss Cicely Haringay braced herself. 'Quite sure.' Picking up the pen she signed the document. As she did so she felt a sinking sensation. With the signing of the document she had sold her beautiful manor house, and for the first time in its 400-year history it had passed out of Haringay hands.

'If I could just ask you to date it?' Mr Weedon prompted her.

Cicely roused herself. 'Of course.' She added the date—25 June, 1904—before handing back the document to Mr Weedon.

'May I say what a pleasure it has been doing business with you?' said the solicitor politely, as he took the proffered document and put it away.

Cicely forced herself to smile. 'Thank you. And thank you for all your help in arranging the sale.'

'Not at all.'

Cicely turned to the door, her business concluded. Then, on a sudden impulse, she looked back at Mr Weedon. 'Mr Evington plans to take up residence at the start of next month, I think you said?'

'He does. He had hoped to take up

residence sooner, but as a city gentleman there are many calls on his time, and he has had to put off the date of his arrival.'

Cicely's smile was fixed. 'Of course.' She wished her smile could have been genuine. It was not Mr Weedon's fault that a cit had bought the Manor. If she had had time, she would have waited for a family to buy it, people who would have fallen in love with the beautiful old house and treated it with the affection it deserved, but her father's death had left her with such pressing debts that she had had to accept the first offer she had received. A generous offer, it was true, but one made by a man who had bought her beloved Manor without even seeing it, as offhandedly as though it had been a bale of cloth or a barrelful of tar.

Still, there was no use repining. She was fortunate to have found a buyer, and she comforted herself with the thought that at least she had not had to sell the Lodge.

Thanking Mr Weedon again she pulled on her gloves and left the office, descending the stairs and reclaiming her bicycle, which she had left propped against the wall outside. Her flat straw hat, calf-length divided skirt, bolero jacket and neat boots were ideally suited to bicycling, and she threw one leg expertly over the saddle before setting off back to the Lodge.

She soon left the town of Oakleigh behind

her. As she cycled along the peaceful country lane she felt her spirits begin to rise. Selling the Manor had been difficult, but still, it was over now, and she had much to be thankful for. She had paid off all her father's debts, and she still had enough money left over to enable her to live in modest comfort.

She turned left at the crossroads and headed towards Little Oakleigh. The summer afternoon was a beautiful one. The rain of the morning had given way to bright sunshine, and she found herself enjoying the ride. High hedges grew at either side of the lane. Grass verges, covered in wild flowers, ran in an untidy profusion alongside, and a rabbit hopped out from a neighbouring field and twitched its nose, before hopping along the verge and disappearing under the hedge again.

She began to draw near the village of Little Oakleigh. Only a mile more to go and she would be at the Lodge. Which was a good thing, she thought, as she heard the chimes of the church clock ringing out over the countryside, because she had invited Alice to tea.

She began to pedal more vigorously. Then, turning a corner, she started the descent to the forge. At the bottom of the hill she applied the brakes, slowing to take the corner. She was just about to make the turn when, coming round the corner, she saw a motor car.

But there aren't any cars in the village! she

thought in alarm.

There was no time for further thought, as she had to swerve to avoid it. She was just congratulating herself on the success of her manoeuvre when she realized to her horror that she was heading straight towards the duck pond, and before she could turn the handlebars again the front wheel struck the edge and she was thrown head over heels into the water.

She lay where she had fallen, too surprised to move. Then she slowly pushed herself into a sitting position. She remained quite still for a minute, with pond water lapping round her, whilst she gathered her wits. It had all happened so quickly that she still had not quite taken it in. She was cold and wet and . . . hurt? Gingerly she stretched out one leg. It felt as though it might be a little bruised, but otherwise it seemed all right. Then she stretched out the other leg. That, too, seemed unhurt. She gave a sigh of relief. She had been lucky, then. Fortunately for her, the pond was lined with a thick layer of mud and weed and, dirty as it was, it had given her a soft landing. The only thing that might have been hurt was her pride, but luckily even that had been spared her, as one glance along the lane showed her that no one had witnessed her tumble.

Slowly she began to pick herself up. Her skirt was waterlogged and she tottered backwards for a moment as she accustomed herself to its weight. Then she regained her balance and stood up straight and felt herself all over. Her arms and head, as well as her legs, seemed to be in one piece, but as she touched her head she realized she had lost her hat.

She scanned the pond. It was nowhere to be seen. She turned round, searching the water behind her, and finally glimpsed the bedraggled item floating just out of reach. Her spirits rose—and then immediately fell. Because there, leaning against his Daimler, which was now parked by the side of the road, was the gentleman who had caused her accident.

She gave an exclamation of vexation. Was it not enough that he had knocked her from her bicycle? Did he really have to stand there and watch as she struggled out of the pond as well?

Adding to her annoyance was the fact that, whilst she was wet and dirty and floundering in the duck pond, he was both clean and dry. Worse still, he was laughing.

'I fail to see what is so amusing,' she remarked haughtily, as she reached for her hat.

Despite her efforts to ignore him, she could not quite manage it. He was about thirty years of age, she guessed, with dark hair, deep brown eyes and a distinctively contoured face. His clothes were smart and fashionable—a pair of narrow trousers, a straight-cut jacket, a light driving coat and a pair of driving gloves— and marked him out as a city dweller.

As if it wasn't enough that she had had to sell her beloved Manor to a cit, she thought, another of the breed had to knock her off her bike. But really, it was hardly surprising. Since the advent of the car, cits had taken to driving out into the country regularly at the weekends, polluting the air with their noxious fumes.

Her anger towards the man who had bought her beloved Manor fuelled her anger towards the gentleman with the Daimler and she spoke with more asperity than usual.

'A country gentleman, having knocked a young lady from her bicycle, would be quick to make amends,' she declared, 'but I suppose such common civilities should not be looked for from a cit.'

At her contemptuous utterance of the word cit he paused in the act of lighting a cigar, which he was holding between his teeth, and his eyes darkened. His hands, which were cupped round the lighted match, froze.

'You, however, would rather content yourself with laughing at your victim,' she went on, not noticing the change in his expression, 'whilst littering the lane with your spent matches,' she finished crossly. This last remark was directed to the match he was holding. Without lighting his cigar, he had shaken it out and was on the point of throwing it away.

A scowl crossed his face. Then suddenly it cleared and a sardonic smile took its place. His hand closed round the spent match and he put it in his pocket.

He has done it to spite me! she thought. Taking no further notice of him she made another attempt to retrieve her hat, which was twirling lazily on the surface of the shallow water. This time she managed to catch it. She picked it up and put it on her head—only to have it unleash a flood of pond water. And just when she had thought her dignity could sink no lower! she reflected, as it cascaded down her face. The sooner she was back at the Lodge again the better.

With this end in mind she waded over to her bicycle, which was sticking out of the mud. She pulled on the handlebars. Nothing happened. She waded round to the other side of the bicycle, her sodden skirt making her movements slow and clumsy, and tried again. But again to no avail.

And then a pair of hands—strong, masculine hands—covered hers.

Cicely froze.

The cit, coming up behind her, had wrapped his arms around her and was proceeding to add his strength to her own.

For a moment she had the most peculiar feeling as a rush of tingles spread outwards from her hands and radiated through her body. Was it a result of the accident? she asked herself. Had she perhaps hurt herself after all? But no, she did not feel hurt. The sensation, whilst being unsettling, was not painful. Quite the opposite, in fact. It was strangely pleasurable. But what was it? It was certainly like nothing she had ever felt before. For some reason it had started when the cit had put his arms around her . . .

Reminded of the liberty he had taken, she said, 'I don't need your help,' completely ignoring the fact she had berated him for the lack of it a few minutes earlier.

'You'll never get your bike out of the mud without it.'

There was a humorous note in his voice, and it roused Cicely's anger. Ignoring his comment she shrugged him off. Then she gave another tug on the handlebars, but again the bicycle refused to move.

His arms came round her again, and she pushed him away. 'When I need your help, I'll ask for it,' she said.

He gave a mocking smile, but nevertheless he stood back.

She was aware of his eyes lingering on her as she struggled with the bicycle and felt herself growing hot and flustered. It was obvious she couldn't manage without his help, and yet she would rather leave her bicycle in the pond and squelch her way home than admit she needed his assistance.

He watched her for another minute, then

said, 'It's no good. I can't stand by and watch you wrestle with it any longer. Like it or not—'

'No,' she snapped. As soon as she had said it she realized how churlish she had sounded, and added ungraciously, 'There is no point in you getting dirty as well.'

There was a sudden silence. From nowhere a cold wind sprang up and blew over the pond.

Then, 'I've been dirtier,' he said.

She did not know how it was, but it was as if her words had unleashed a sudden bitterness in him; as though they had somehow opened an old wound she could not possibly understand. But it was gone as quickly as it had arrived.

'Wait at the side of the pond,' he commanded, wading into the water again. 'That way I don't have to worry about splashing you.'

'It's a pity you weren't so concerned about splashing me when you raced through the village,' she returned, ignoring the arrogance of his command. She looked down at her ruined cycling clothes. She sighed. 'You cits have no idea how to behave in the country. You race along with no concern for anyone else. But I suppose I should be thankful,' she finished. 'At least I wasn't killed.'

'Four miles an hour isn't exactly racing,' he pointed out with a mocking light in his eyes. 'In fact, you were going far more quickly than I was. With the reckless way you were careering down the hill it's a miracle you didn't kill us both.'

'Are you always so infuriating?' she asked in exasperation, turning to face him.

He smiled wickedly. 'So I've been told. But I can't help having a lively sense of the ridiculous.'

'Ridiculous?' The atmosphere changed, and Cicely's face took on a deceptively innocent expression. 'You are saying I look ridiculous?'

The words dropped into the silence with the mildness of a lamb.

But the quirk of his mouth showed that he had not been deceived. His eyes gleamed with barely suppressed amusement.

'Ah! Now you've caught me. If I say yes, I confirm you in your belief that I'm a city gent with no manners. And if I say no . . .' She raised her eyebrows, waiting for him to finish his sentence.

But it was no good. Try as he might he could not help laughing. 'I've already answered one of your questions. Now you answer one of mine: if you weren't so angry, wouldn't you be laughing, too?'

An unwilling smile tugged at the corner of Cicely's mouth as she had a sudden vision of herself, wet and bedraggled, with pond weed sticking out of her hair. So absurd was the picture that she almost succumbed to laughter. But she fought it down. Laughing would only make his manners worse. She straightened her shoulders. 'Certainly not,' she said repressively. 'The sight of someone in distress has never amused me. Now, if you will kindly retrieve my bicycle, I will be on my way.'

He shrugged. 'As you wish.'

Cicely splashed her way to the edge of the pond. She would have preferred to retrieve her bicycle herself, but she had realized it was impossible. That being so, she would have to let the gentleman help her. She climbed out of the pond. Water trickled from her sodden garments, making a puddle on the grass. She took a deep breath and then set about wringing her skirt as best she could. Luckily, being specially designed for bicycling, it was only mid-calf length, and therefore much easier to deal with than a floor-length skirt would have been. Having wrung out her skirt, she straightened her jacket before re-settling her hat on top of her ash-blonde head. Then she looked round to see how the gentleman was doing. He had managed to rescue her bicycle and was in the process of carrying it to the side of the pond. But it was in a sorry state.

'Oh, no!' Cicely wailed. The once-gleaming machine was covered in pond slime. Mud was caught between the spokes, and the handlebars were bent.

'It's not as bad as it looks,' he said. There was still a glint of humour in his eye, but there was a hint of something softer as well, and his mouth was surprisingly gentle.

11

'Not to you, perhaps,' she remarked with a sigh. 'The next time you go for a jaunt,' she went on, taking it from him, 'I suggest you choose a different village. Little Oakleigh is a peaceful place, and we prefer it to remain that way.'

Then, filled with a sudden longing to be safely back at the Lodge, she mounted her bicycle and, without a backward glance, she rode away.

The gentleman looked after her for a minute. There was something very appealing about her, even though she was covered in mud. Her carriage was erect, revealing the beautiful line of her straight back. Her neck was elegant, and there was a graceful set to her head. Her hair, bedraggled though it was, had a softness about it that made him long to touch it, and the tendrils that had escaped from their pins were being blown across her shoulders in the most tantalizing way. Her slender curves, not quite hidden beneath her bolero jacket, together with the glimpse of shapely calf afforded by her bicycling skirt made his body stir. It was a long time since anyone had so attracted him.

But becoming attracted to one of the local girls was not on his agenda.

Against his will he watched her until she was out of sight, then climbed back into his Daimler and started up the engine.

He pulled away and began to drive carefully

12

on towards Oakleigh Manor. He was mindful of the fact that at any moment another young lady on a bicycle might come hurtling round a corner before launching herself into a ditch!

It was not an auspicious start to his new life as lord of the manor, he reflected with a wry smile, but things could have been worse. He could have been confronted by an angry matron—or worse still, by Miss Cicely Haringay. Miss Haringay, from what he could make out, was a determined spinster who spent her life running Sunday schools and engaging in charitable works. He knew the type: a monstrous battle-axe with a ramrod back and enormous bosom who liked nothing better than telling everyone else what to do. But instead, he had been confronted by a slight, appealing girl and he found he was looking forward to meeting her again. For all her high-and-mighty manner, there had been something very engaging about her.

Reluctantly, he brought his thoughts back to the present. He needed his wits about him if he was to remember the directions he had been given and arrive safely at the Manor. He drove on for a while, but by and by his face began to settle into a frown. He had the feeling he had gone too far and overshot the mark. A few minutes later he was sure of it. He was in the village no longer, but heading out towards open countryside. There was nothing for it. He would have to turn round and try again.

He drove more slowly this time, his eyes searching for any sign of the Manor. It was barely visible from the road, his agent had said, but a lodge and a pair of fine gates gave evidence of its position. At last he saw the Lodge, a neat, square building, and began to edge the Daimler forward more confidently. Yes, that was it. He reached the gates and turned into a long drive which wound between acres of verdant lawns. Despite himself, he was impressed. Although he might not have bought the Manor with the intention of making it his home, he still could not help admiring the sweeping lawns, the venerable trees and the herd of deer that grazed peacefully in the dappled sunlight beneath them.

Another bend of the drive and he caught sight of the house itself. It was far more sprawling than he had imagined, and presented a hotch-potch appearance, as though successive generations of Haringays had added to it, each in the style of their own era. A Tudor wing adjoined the main section, which appeared to be in the Georgian style, whilst a turret at the corner rose fantastically into the sky and spoke of the recently departed Victorian age. But despite its hotch-potch appearance—or perhaps because of it—it had a warm and welcoming feel.

In another few minutes he pulled up in front of Oakleigh Manor. His eye wandered up an impressive flight of steps that led to the front door. At the top of the steps was Roddy.

'What kept you? Car trouble?'

Roddy, Alex's younger brother, ran down the stone steps and cast his eye over the motor. He was a smart young man of four-and-twenty years of age. He was fashionably dressed in a straight-cut jacket and a pair of trousers with knife-sharp creases. His hair was sandy and his face good-humoured. 'You were supposed to be here half an hour ago.'

'The motor's fine.' Alex got out of the car, closing the door with a satisfying *thunk*! 'I had a slight accident, that's all.'

'You haven't scratched the paintwork?' asked Roddy anxiously, running his eyes over the bodywork: Alex's Daimler was, to Roddy, the height of desirability.

Alex raised one dark eyebrow. 'Of course not. What do you take me for? Strictly speaking, I wasn't the one who had the accident—although I didn't escape unscathed,' he said, as they walked up the steps. He glanced down at his trousers, which were wet and muddy round the bottom of each leg.

'If not you, who then?' asked Roddy, taking in Alex's wet trousers with amusement.

'It was a young lady. A bicyclist. She came careering down the hill by the forge and almost crashed into me as she rounded the corner. It was only by some efficient manoeuvring that she managed to avoid the

15

car . . .'

Roddy breathed a sigh of relief. 'No harm done, then.'

'I wouldn't quite say that,' laughed Alex, taking off his driving gloves as they went into the Manor. 'She ended up in the duck pond!'

'Not hurt, I hope?' asked Roddy.

'Would I be laughing if she was? No, of course not. The only thing she hurt was her pride. Of which she seemed to have more than her fair share.'

'I hope she wasn't anyone important. The success of our scheme lies in your being accepted here. You need the goodwill of your neighbours, don't forget. They have to want to attend your gatherings, and more than that, they have to want to attend them decked out in all their finery. Otherwise there will be nothing to tempt the thief to strike again.'

'Which is our only hope of catching him. I know.' He thought. 'She didn't look important,' he said. He divested himself of his car coat, which had protected his narrow trousers and straight-cut jacket from the dust of the road. 'Fine grey eyes, a determined chin, and a tantalizing figure. Probably just a girl from the village.'

'Let's hope so,' said Roddy. 'Well, what do you think?' he asked, changing the subject, as he looked round the empty but beautiful hall.

'It's a fine old place,' said Alex. He, too, looked round the hall. It was light and bright,

16

and with its cream walls it had a pleasantly cool and spacious feel. Although it was at present bare—no paintings or portraits lined the staircase, and no console tables or other items of furniture took away from the emptiness—the proportions were elegant, and the tall windows let in plenty of daylight. He turned round slowly, taking it in. An imposing staircase led upwards. He let his eyes return to the ground floor. A number of doors, half open, led into different rooms. He walked across the hall, his footsteps echoing on the wooden floor. He threw open the first door. A large, high-ceilinged room was revealed, with windows looking out over the front of the house. This room was not entirely empty. A few pieces of good furniture—an impressive mahogany dining-table and chairs, and a mahogany sideboard—remained. Alex looked enquiringly at Roddy.

'Miss Haringay had to let some of the furniture remain with the house,' he explained. 'She did not have room to take it all to the Lodge.'

Alex nodded. He cast his eye round the room once more. 'It's very impressive,' he said, before wandering back into the hall and looking round again. 'Garson chose well.'

'I still think you should have looked it over yourself before buying it.'

'What for? Garson's an efficient agent. He knew what I was looking for—an imposing residence in the right area. It's not as though I wanted to call the place home.'

'I suppose so,' said Roddy. 'It needs modernizing, of course.'

'It does. But as I don't propose to live here permanently that isn't a consideration. What matters is that it's of the right stature, and it's in the right place. Which it is.' His glance ran round the hall once again, and then suddenly his voice took on a steely quality. 'Once it's baited it will make the perfect trap.'

*   *   *

Cicely propped her bicycle up against the wall of the Lodge. Much of the mud had been dislodged on the journey home, and she knew that a good dousing with the watering can would restore it to most of its former glory. The handlebars she had already managed to bend back into shape. They had not been badly damaged, fortunately, and it had been an easy matter to put them straight.

She went down the garden to the shed and fetched the watering can and then cleaned the bicycle herself. Gibson had enough to do, without cleaning her bicycle as well.

Having successfully carried out her task she left her bicycle drying in the warm June sunshine and went into the house. Avoiding Gibson, her butler, who had refused to leave her service no matter how impecunious she had become, she made her way up to the bedroom where she stripped off her wet things. Her short black boots were first, followed by her fawn gaiters, which she unbuttoned with the help of a button hook. Then came her divided skirt, her drawers, her shirt and her chemise. They would have to be cleaned, but that was a problem for later on. Right now, she wanted to clean herself. She ran a bath, thankful of the fact that the Lodge had had plumbing installed in one of her father's rare bursts of enthusiasm for something other than his beloved bicycles. But she noted with a sigh that the range must not be working properly as the water was not very hot. Still, it would have to do. Slipping into the tepid water she gave both herself and her hair a thorough wash before dressing herself in fresh, clean clothes.

Unlike most other young ladies of one-and-twenty, Cicely did not have a maid, and in fact had never had one. Her dear father had had very little idea about a young lady's needs, and her mother, alas, had died when she had been a young child. And since her father's death, Cicely had discovered that his unworldliness had resulted in a mountain of debts, so that she had been unable to hire one. As a result, by dint of choosing the most suitable clothes, she had grown proficient in the art of dressing and undressing herself.

She slipped on a clean pair of lace-trimmed

knickers and a fashionable bosom amplifier—a pretty camisole with row upon row of tiny frills sewn across the front to give the impression that she possessed a modishly voluptuous chest—followed by a lace-trimmed petticoat. Just for a moment she was thankful she did not have a maid. If she had had a maid, she would have felt obliged to wear a whalebone corset, but without assistance she could not possibly put one on.

Taking a white blouse with a lace corsage out of the wardrobe she matched it with a lilac skirt. It was long and flowing, fitting closely over her slender hips before belling out at the ankle, whereupon it trailed along behind her in the most delightful way.

She was fortunate that she had some good clothes, she reflected. With any luck, they would last her for the next few years.

She had just finished dressing, and was busily towelling dry her hair, when she caught sight of Alice through the window. Good! Alice was right on time.

Within minutes, Alice, a childhood friend who came and went as though she was one of the family, entered her bedroom.

'Such news,' said Alice without preamble, throwing herself down on the bed. 'You'll never guess—goodness, Cicely, what happened to your clothes?'

Cicely gave a sigh. It seemed she was fated not to be able to keep the incident to herself. 'I had an accident. I fell off my bicycle.'

'That's not like you,' said Alice with a frown.

'It wasn't my fault.' Cicely's desire to confide in her friend overcame her pride. 'I was coming down the hill by the forge and I'd just turned the corner when I saw a motor car right in front of me. I had to swerve to avoid a crash, and I ended up in the duck pond.' It was too much. The memory of the accident, now that she was dry and fresh and safely back at the Lodge, was so ridiculous that she had to laugh.

'Oh, Cicely, how awful!' laughed Alice. 'You must have looked a sorry sight!'

'I was drenched. There was water everywhere. And pond weed. It was sticking out of my hair! And when I rescued my hat and put it on—'

'Don't tell me. The water poured down your face! Oh, Cicely! How dreadful. I wish I'd been there!'

'I'm glad you weren't! It was bad enough that that man—' She stopped short.

'Man?' Alice looked at her enquiringly and then broke out laughing again. 'You don't mean to say that someone saw you like that?'

Cicely pulled a face. 'The driver of the car.'

'How awful!' laughed Alice, torn between amusement and horror. 'What did he say?'

'He didn't say anything. He laughed at me!'

'What a cad.'

'And so I told him, in no uncertain terms. "A country gentleman, having knocked a young lady from her bicycle, would be quick to make amends", I informed him, "but I suppose such common civilities should not be looked for from a cit".' Her mouth quirked.

'Oh, Cicely, you didn't!' Alice collapsed into laughter again.

'I did.'

'You mean, you didn't laugh?' asked Alice, pulling herself together.

'Of course not—although at one point I was tempted. But I was too cross. He had knocked me from my bicycle and then he had laughed at me. I wasn't going to give him the satisfaction of joining in.'

Alice's face was sympathetic. 'You poor dear. Did anyone else see you—apart from the monster, that is?'

Cicely had a brief vision of the owner of the motor car: dark hair, athletic build, long legs and an infuriatingly mocking smile. A monster? No, he hadn't been a monster. Unaccountably, the strange sensation she had experienced when he had put his arms round her, the tingling feeling, which had made her body feel strangely alive, came back to her. She shook herself in an effort to drive it away.

No, he hadn't been a monster, she thought again. More's the pity. Because if he had been a monster, his laughter would have been so much easier to bear . . .

'No one else, thank goodness,' she said, answering Alice's question. 'I was sure I would bump into someone in the village, but fortunately I managed to get back here without seeing a soul.'

'That's a relief! If the village boys had seen you you would never have heard the end of it. But now, tell me, how did the rest of your afternoon go?'

Cicely sank down on the bed. She felt deflated suddenly, as though the events of the early afternoon had finally caught up with her. Rousing herself, she said at last, 'As well as can be expected. I cycled over to Oakleigh and signed the final document as arranged, and then I cycled back again.'

'It was very brave of you to sell the Manor,' said Alice. She put her hand consolingly on Cicely's arm. 'I don't think I could have done it.'

Cicely sighed. 'I had no choice, in the end. The debts were too large. Selling the Manor was the only way to pay them. Father was a dear, but he was always so absent-minded. I always knew it, of course, but I didn't realize at the time just quite how bad he was. I'd always assumed he paid the bills, at least, but when he died I realized he hadn't paid anything for years. He always meant to, I'm sure, but he simply forgot about them five minutes after they'd arrived.'

'His head was always full of some

enthusiasm or other—usually bicycles,' said Alice.

Cicely smiled. 'Yes. He loved them. They were his passion. "Velocipedes", he used to call them—although "boneshakers" is a better description, if you ask me. He loved riding them, collecting them, inventing them . . .' She gave a sigh as she thought of her dearly loved but completely impractical father, who had died the preceding year. Then she rallied herself. 'But still, it's done now. The Manor is sold, the papers are signed, and I am busy settling into my new life at the Lodge.'

There was a pause in the conversation. Alice stood up and strolled round the room. She stopped in front of Cicely's dressing-table. She picked up Cicely's silver-backed hairbrush, before putting it down and picking up the hand mirror, then putting that down and picking up the hairbrush once more. Without looking at Cicely she asked nonchalantly, 'How would you feel if the new owner was to arrive earlier than expected?'

'Earlier?' Cicely's eyebrows rose. 'How much earlier?'

'Oh . . .' Alice hesitated. Then she put down the hairbrush with a clatter. 'The thing is, Cicely,' she said in a rush, 'it turns out he's already here.'

'Mr Evington? Here?' asked Cicely, horror-struck. 'Oh, no. He can't be.' But one look at Alice's face convinced her it was true. 'Are you sure?' she demanded, wondering suddenly whether Alice could be mistaken. 'He's not meant to be here until the start of next month.'

Alice nodded. 'Quite sure. He changed his mind about waiting, that's all. But he's definitely here. Mrs Sealyham's seen him, and she told me all about him.' She added nonchalantly, 'He's young, handsome, and charming, she says.'

'Mrs Sealyham thinks every bachelor is young, handsome and charming,' returned Cicely.

'Even so.' Alice paused. 'Wouldn't it be wonderful if he really is?'

'Why?' asked Cicely.

'Because . . . because then you could marry him,' Alice said. 'And you could go back to the Manor and raise your children there, as you always wanted to.'

Cicely's eyebrows rose in astonishment. 'Marry Alex Evington? The man who bought my beloved Manor as though it was no more important than a loaf of bread?' His casual attitude to the purchase of her beautiful home still hurt. 'Goodness, Alice, whatever can you be thinking of? I can't imagine anything worse. He has neither feelings nor sensitivity. He is a brash businessman who sees everything in terms of profit and loss—a typical cit, in fact. He doesn't see the Manor as a home, but as a possession. He is the last man in the world I would ever want to marry.'

'You might change your mind once you meet him,' said Alice. Cicely laughed.

And pigs might fly!'

CHAPTER TWO

'Ready to face the Gorgon in her lair?' asked Roddy with a twinkle in his eye.

It was the following morning, and he and Alex were talking over the breakfast-table.

The dining-room in which they were eating was an elegantly proportioned room with high ceilings and elaborate plaster mouldings, giving evidence of its Georgian origins. It was painted in a pale shade of biscuit which, despite its shabbiness, gave the room a pleasant feel. Tall windows flooded the room with light. Long fawn curtains, topped with shaped pelmets, were swept back to reveal the splendid view. The gravel path beneath the window was dotted with weeds, it was true, and the lawns beyond it were unkempt, but across the ha-ha, that useful ditch which separated the house from the park and prevented the animals from wandering too close, the deer at least kept the grass short. Above them large oaks, fully leaved, rippled in the breeze.

'Ready,' said Alex, looking up from his meal. 'As soon as I've finished my breakfast, I am going to visit Miss Cicely Haringay.'

'I'm glad to see you're building up your strength.' Roddy looked meaningfully at Alex's plate of bacon, sausages, mushrooms, tomatoes and fried eggs.

Alex laughed. 'Something tells me I'm going to need it. Charitable spinsters are not my favourite people, and charitable spinsters who were born with silver spoons in their mouths . . .' He let the sentence tail away.

'She may not be so bad,' said Roddy. He spread a thick layer of marmalade on his toast.

'Oh, no? She's already interfered with my running of the Manor, and I haven't even met her yet.'

'How on earth has she done that?' asked Roddy, pausing with his piece of toast halfway to his mouth.

'By customarily allowing the Sunday school children to hold their annual picnic on my lawns. I had a visit from a Mrs Murgatroyd yesterday afternoon,' he explained to Roddy, 'shortly after I arrived. She told me—told me, mind you, didn't ask me—that the Sunday school picnic, which is in a few weeks' time, will be held, as usual, at the Manor. And when I told her that it might not be convenient she fixed me with a gimlet eye and said the Haringays had always allowed the Sunday school children to hold their picnic here, and that she knew Miss Haringay would be most put out if the custom did not continue.'

Roddy laughed. 'You'll have to expect some

27

of that sort of thing, you know,' he said reasonably.

'But I don't have to like it. Nor do I have to like the idea of mixing with the Mrs Murgatroyds of this world.'

'Was she really that bad?'

'Worse. I've no use for her kind. They're rich and idle, and they think they have the right to order everyone else's lives. It would be bad enough if their own lives were perfect, but they're not. Far from it. The landed classes have all kinds of faults. They run up debts and never bother paying their bills—Haringay's a prime example. The man's family had lived here for time out of mind, but did that mean he paid his way? No. He thought he was too good for such things, I've no doubt, like the rest of his kind. Bought everything on credit, and the poor shopkeepers who supplied his goods were put out of business, most likely.'

'Be fair. You don't know Haringay put anyone out of business.'

'And you don't know he didn't,' returned Alex.

'And anyway, his daughter can't be so bad,' said Roddy, between mouthfuls of toast. 'She *did* pay all his debts when he died. That's why she had to sell the Manor.'

'And was mighty glad to get rid of it, I shouldn't wonder.' He looked round the beautiful but neglected room. The paintwork was shabby and in the far corner it had peeled

28

off, whilst round the fireplace it had become discoloured with smoke from the coal fire. The windows, having shrunk and expanded many times over the centuries with the damp and the heat, did not fit properly and rattled gently in the breeze. 'It's a draughty great barn of a place with no modern conveniences. Miss Cicely Haringay knew what she was doing when she sold the Manor. She got rid of a white elephant and settled herself snugly in the Lodge.'

He turned his attention back to his breakfast.

'I hope you were polite to her. Mrs What's-her-name from the Sunday school, I mean,' said Roddy, reaching for another piece of toast.

'Mrs Murgatroyd? Yes, I was polite. Though it stuck in my throat to be polite to someone like that.' He grimaced. 'She's exactly the sort of woman who made Katie's life such a misery when she was in service.' His face softened momentarily as he thought of his younger sister. At one time she had been branded a thief by the landed classes. Now, fortunately, she had been safely rescued from service by Alex's hard-earned money. 'And exactly the kind who were so eager to believe ill of Katie. When I think of the way that cur framed her . . .' He broke off in exasperation, remembering the way in which the Honourable Martin Goss, having stolen a valuable bracelet, had dropped it into Katie's apron once its loss had been discovered, in order to divert suspicion from himself. He had deliberately thrown the blame on an innocent parlour-maid who had had no one to stand up for her, and who had been thrown out on to the streets as a result. Alex took a minute to calm himself, then he went on, 'But we'll catch him, Roddy. We'll nab him red-handed. We'll show him up for the liar and thief he is.'

'And to that end, you'll have to be nice to Miss Haringay,' Roddy reminded him. 'Charm her. Win her over. We need her on our side. If she accepts us, then the rest of the county will do the same. They'll be delighted to come to our balls and entertainments, and then we have only to tempt the thief with the kind of jewels he likes and we have him.'

Alex pushed away his empty plate. 'You're right. What does eating a little humble pie matter if it means we catch the man who blamed Katie for the theft of that wretched bracelet? I'll be as charming as the day is long to Miss Haringay, and I won't return until she's promised to come to our first ball.'

*　　　*　　　*

Cicely was in the kitchen of the Lodge, looking at the range. It was a large, black contraption which at the moment reminded her of a sleeping dragon. Which was a pity, because what she really wanted to see was an angry dragon, all heat and fire and dancing flames. Because then, and only then, would she be able to get some hot water and have a proper bath.

The range was, without doubt, the most contrary thing she had ever encountered in her life. And yet the range at the Manor had always been so obedient. Mrs Crannock, the cook, had never had any trouble with it, and had made the most delicious meals on it. But the range at the Lodge seemed to have a mind of its own.

'I've tried everything I can think of, miss,' said Gibson unhappily, 'but it won't heat the water properly and it keeps going out.'

'What did Mrs Crannock used to do?' Cicely felt as helpless as Gibson in the face of the uncooperative range.

'I don't rightly know, miss,' said Gibson. He drew himself up a little as he spoke.

'Of course not,' said Cicely soothingly. She realized that she had, unwittingly, ruffled Gibson's feathers. At the Manor, Gibson had been a person of consequence. As the Haringays' butler he had been at the top of the servants' hierarchy, and it would have been beneath his dignity to enquire into such menial matters. 'If only Mrs Crannock was still at the Manor we could ask her—although I suspect it would have been the job of the scullery maid to see to the range. Still, Mrs Crannock, I am sure, would have known what to do. But Mr Evington has brought his own servants down from the city with him and Mrs Crannock has taken a well-deserved position with Lord Boothlake so she is no longer here for us to ask.'

'No, miss,' said Gibson.

Cicely looked helplessly at the range. 'We must have hot water. There's a copperload of clothes to be washed, and on top of that we will need the range if we are to have a hot meal.' She picked up the poker and, opening the small door at the front of the range, she poked hopefully at the coals. 'It is worse than I thought,' she said. 'There is no spark at all. It has completely gone out. Well, we must simply light it again. You pump the bellows, Gibson, whilst I get it alight.'

'Very good, miss,' said Gibson.

Ten minutes later, Cicely at last succeeded in lighting the range. Gibson pumped manfully with the bellows and the small glow began to grow larger until the range was well and truly alight.

Cicely gave a sigh of relief and straightened up, pushing a strand of ash-blonde hair out of her eyes. Keeping her hair in its fashionable pompadour style was not easy when she had so much work to do. Stray strands would keep working free of their pins and falling in soft tendrils around her face.

She had just pushed it back into place,

unknowingly smudging her cheek with soot at the same time, when there came a knock at the front door.

'Are you at home, miss?' asked Gibson. He slipped on his frock coat and prepared to answer the door.

'Yes, Gibson,' said Cicely. 'I will go through into the sitting-room. You may show the visitor in there.' She went over to the sink and washed her sooty hands, shaking off the excess water and drying them thoroughly on one of the kitchen towels before going into the sitting-room.

The sitting-room was a pretty apartment at the back of the house. It was well-proportioned, though far smaller than anything Cicely had been used to at the Manor, and had a variety of nooks and alcoves which gave it character and charm. French windows looked out over the gardens and filled the room with light. A faded sofa was set in front of the windows with another one facing it. A collection of inlaid console tables, brought from the Manor, were arranged artistically, and the far wall was adorned by a fireplace.

It will be Mrs Murgatroyd, thought Cicely as she settled herself down on the sofa. She will have come to talk to me about the arrangements for the Sunday school picnic.

But as the door opened, it was not Mrs Murgatroyd who walked in, it was the gentleman who had knocked her from her bicycle!

Cicely's eyes opened wide in astonishment. The cit? Here? In her sitting-room?

He was looking every bit as attractive as he had looked the day before. His clothes, smartly cut—the trousers with their turned-up cuffs, and the jacket open to reveal the fob-strewn waistcoat—showed off the lean yet muscular build of his body. His dark-brown hair was cut short, accentuating the strongly defined planes of his face, and was shot through with gleams of chestnut. His eyes were a velvety brown, and something about the way he looked at her gave her the most peculiar feeling inside . . .

But this would not do, she chided herself. She was allowing her thoughts to run away with her. She needed to gather her wits, for with this provoking man she knew she would need them.

And yet, perhaps not. For on seeing her he stopped dead, and looked just as surprised as she was.

'I was looking for Miss Haringay,' he said uncertainly, turning to Gibson.

'Thank you, Gibson,' said Cicely quickly. She did not know what the cit was doing in her sitting-room but she decided to send Gibson away as quickly as possible. She had no desire for any of the distressing details of her previous encounter with him—or with the duck pond!—to leak out.

Gibson, his mouth open in the act of announcing the visitor, closed it again. 'Very good, miss,' he murmured, and backed out of the room.

'My apologies,' said the cit. His eyes flashed, sending a shiver up and down Cicely's spine, and a wicked smile touched his mouth. 'I seem to have come to the wrong house. I was looking for Miss Haringay.'

'I am Miss Haringay,' she said, standing up. She did not know why, but she felt she would be better able to hold her own if she was standing. But what on earth could he wish to see her about? Did he want to apologize, perhaps, for his earlier rude behaviour?

'Miss *Cicely* Haringay,' he said, as if to make the matter clear. Already he was turning to walk out of the room.

'There is only one Miss Haringay,' she said, 'and I am she.'

'*You* are Miss Haringay?'

His face broke into a sudden grin, and Cicely flushed. She had hoped he would make no reference to her accident, but it seemed from his grin that it was uppermost in his mind, for what else could be causing him such amusement?

Just for a moment she wondered why his eyes kept straying to a fixed point on her cheek, but then dismissed the thought, the better to concentrate on the matter in hand.

'Do you always laugh at young ladies?' she

asked, trying to hide her discomfort by speaking sharply. 'Or is it only me?'

'I was not laughing at you,' he said, but his eyes were dancing as he spoke. 'I was just laughing at—'

He raised his hand as he was speaking and Cicely had the unaccountable feeling he was going to stroke her face. She took a step backwards. For some reason the thought of him stroking her face made her shiver. Though it was hardly surprising, she told herself, as his behaviour was entirely unpredictable and she must make him remember his manners. 'Yes?' she asked quellingly.

'Oh . . .' He seemed to think better of whatever it was he had been about to do. 'Nothing,' he said, dropping his hand.

And what is your business here?' she asked. 'I take it you had a reason for calling?'

'Indeed I did. I wanted to introduce myself . . .'

Not to apologize, but to introduce himself! she thought, startled. Whatever next?

'And invite you to a ball.'

Her eyes flew open in astonishment. A *ball*?

She glanced at the door, wondering how long it would take Gibson to enter the room and eject this strange gentleman, for he seemed to have run mad.

'You don't need to call for your butler,' he said, his eyes dancing again as if he could read her mind. 'I'm not a Bedlamite, and I haven't

36

wandered in off the streets for the purpose of asking you to an imaginary dance, if that's what you're thinking. I'm Alex Evington. I have bought the Manor. We are neighbours, Miss Haringay, and I am here to make your acquaintance—and, of course, to invite you to my house-warming ball.' He went on to explain. 'I wanted to get to know my neighbours, and holding a ball seemed the best way of doing it.'

'Mr Evington?' asked Cicely faintly. Things were getting worse and worse.

'Yes. Had you not guessed?'

'How could I?' She sank back onto the sofa. 'You were not expected until the start of next month'—she frowned—'although I had heard you had changed your plans.' She wondered now why she had not thought of it before: the man who had knocked her from her bicycle was of course the same man who had so carelessly bought her beloved Manor. It was all of a piece, she thought, her eyes hardening slightly. Mr Evington was a man of neither feelings nor sensitivity.

He stood looking down at her with an amused air. 'Is it such a terrible shock?'

Cicely could see nothing amusing in what she had said, and could not think why his eyes kept drifting to her cheek. However, she noticed that he was still standing, and remembering her manners she bid him sit down. If he was indeed Alex Evington then, however disinclined she might be to treat him politely, she would have to do it.

He sat down opposite her, putting his hat on a side table.

The action gave her time to recover her composure.

'I take it you will accept my invitation?' he asked, looking her in the eye.

Cicely pulled herself together. 'Oh, no, I'm afraid that's out of the question.'

'Might I ask why?' he enquired, eyebrows raised.

'I don't see that it's any of your—' she began, before stopping herself. *I don't see that it's any of your business,* she had been going to say, nettled that once again he seemed to be amused at her expense, but realized belatedly that it would be rude. For some reason he seemed to provoke her to rudeness. 'That is, I'm afraid I have a prior engagement,' she said.

'But you don't know when the ball's to be held,' he pointed out.

Cicely flushed. She had been so determined to refuse that she had blurted out a reply without giving it any thought, and he had pounced on the weakness in her argument. She should have taken her time and given him a more convincing excuse, but she had been caught unawares and had wanted to scotch the idea of her attending the ball at once. The one thing she did not want to do was to visit her beloved Manor now that it was no longer her home. If it had been bought by some nice, kindly family who would have loved it and taken care of it, it would have been difficult enough, but when it had been bought by someone with no feelings for it, someone who had bought it as though it was nothing but a commodity . . . no, that was something she could not bear.

And so now she would have to think of a reason to stand by her refusal.

'My diary is fully booked,' she said, thinking quickly. But she could see he was not convinced. There was a grimness about his mouth, and his eyes had become hard. Although why he should be so hostile simply because she had refused an invitation to a ball she could not imagine.

She was soon to find out.

'Would that be because I'm a cit?' He spoke with deceptive politeness, but she was not fooled. There was something watchful about him, something hard and predatory. His body was tense, and beneath his even tone of voice was a note of steel.

'No . . . no, of course not,' she replied, flustered.

'Why of course not?' he asked, with the same hard look in his eyes. 'I believe the landed classes look down on those who've made their money through honest work, instead of having had it fall into their laps on the day of their birth.'

'You forget, Mr Evington, you are one of the landed classes now,' she replied. 'Be careful how you speak of them, lest you blacken your own character along with theirs.'

'I beg your pardon,' he said, with barely concealed anger.

'I doubt if you have ever begged for anything in your life,' she returned, nettled by the angry gleam in his eye, and by the rudeness concealed beneath his polite words.

'Oh, you are mistaken there,' he said; and for a moment she had a glimpse of something much deeper than the well-dressed cit who drove through the village knocking young ladies from their bicycles. It reminded her of another similar change of atmosphere the previous day, when he had been about to pull her bicycle out of the mud, and had said, 'I've been dirtier'. She had the strange feeling there was more to Mr Evington than met the eye.

There was an uncomfortable silence.

'Well, Mr Evington,' said Cicely at last, her voice sounding unnaturally loud in the stillness. 'You have made my acquaintance and issued your invitation. If there is nothing further, I have some letters to write.'

She spoke awkwardly, feeling she was being rude to dismiss him in such a hasty manner, but knowing that she was not equal to continuing the conversation. There was something about Mr Alex Evington that she found profoundly disturbing, and she did not trust herself to be in his company another minute.

She went over to the mantelpiece and pulled the bell.

'Letters?' he enquired. His eyes roved over her face, and to her annoyance, once again he gave an amused smile. Still, at least it lightened the atmosphere. 'Of course,' he said.

He stood up, and for a disturbing moment she thought he was going to cross the room and take her hands. But instead he made no move towards her.

'I must warn you, though, I have not accepted your refusal. I am a stubborn man, Miss Haringay,' he said, picking up his hat.

'In that we are alike,' she retorted, as Gibson entered the room. 'Mr Evington is just leaving, Gibson,' she said.

'Very good, miss.'

Mr Evington made her a bow. 'Miss Haringay.'

And then, turning, he followed Gibson out of the room.

Cicely sank on to the sofa. She felt as though she had just been involved in a sparring match, instead of a formal visit. There was something very disturbing about Mr Evington. He was like no one she had ever met. He did not behave like a cit, nor yet like a country gentleman, and she did not know what to make of him. He seemed to resent the landed classes on the one hand, and yet by buying the Manor he had become one of them on the other. It was most strange.

Strange, too, was the effect he had on her. And not only by setting her skin tingling in the most disconcerting way, but by causing her to forget her manners. She had had a lot of training at keeping a civil tongue in her head, whatever the situation—she had been involved in many charitable works around the village, and was an active supporter of the Sunday school, and whilst she did not always see eye to eye with the other ladies and gentlemen who were involved in the schemes, she always managed to be polite. And yet with Mr Evington she found it almost impossible. Was it because he was always laughing at her? she wondered.

She thought inconsequentially of the way his eyes flashed with wicked humour. It made them almost unbearably attractive, and set her insides to dancing in the most alarming, and yet strangely pleasurable, way.

She quickly berated herself for the thought. He might be young, handsome and charming, as Mrs Sealyham had said, but he was still the man who had bought her beloved Manor without so much as visiting it first. And he was still the man who had knocked her from her bicycle and then laughed at her predicament. And laughed at her again, in her own home, she thought crossly, as she remembered his

42

behaviour that very morning.

One thing was certain, amidst all her confusing thoughts and feelings: Mr Evington was a man to be avoided.

She was just about to return to the kitchen when the door opened and Alice showed herself into the room.

Alice was looking particularly well this morning. Her grey panelled skirt swirled about her ankles, and she was wearing a becoming lace-frilled blouse.

'Have you got one?' she asked, without preamble.

'Got one what?' asked Cicely inelegantly, not immediately guessing what Alice was talking about.

'An invitation. To Mr Evington's ball,' cried Alice.

'No. I haven't,' said Cicely.

'I'm sure you will. It's probably on its way here even now.'

'I shouldn't think so,' said Cicely. 'You see, I don't need one. Mr Evington has just been here, and he asked me to the ball himself.'

'You've seen him?' demanded Alice, eyes wide. 'Well? What's he like?'

She threw herself on to one of the sofas and looked at Cicely expectantly.

'He is the most infuriating man I have ever met,' said Cicely with a sigh. 'He seems to spend his time either insulting me or laughing at me. I could understand him laughing at me yesterday, although I didn't like it—'

'Yesterday?' demanded Alice.

Cicely gave a wry smile. 'Mr Evington is the man who knocked me off my bicycle.'

'Oh, no!' exclaimed Alice.

'Oh, yes. As I say, I could understand him laughing at me yesterday—although it was extremely rude—but today there was no excuse. It is very difficult to have a conversation with a man whose face keeps breaking into an amused smile.'

'Well, you can hardly blame him,' said Alice, giving a smile of her own.

'Not you too, Alice,' said Cicely in exasperation. 'What is wrong with everyone lately?'

'I think you need to look in the mirror.'

Cicely's eyes widened in surprise. Then she walked over to the mantelpiece, above which hung a looking-glass. As soon as she glanced into it she saw the smudge of soot on her face.

'Oh, no!' she exclaimed. 'Odious man! Why didn't he say something?' Then remembered that he had tried, and that he had even been going to wipe the smut away, but that she had prevented him. She sighed. 'Why is it that I have never fallen in the duck pond before, and never had a smudge of soot on my face, and yet as soon as Mr Evington arrives at the Manor I suffer both calamities?' she asked as she took out her handkerchief and rubbed the smudge from her cheek.

44

'Poor Cicely!' laughed Alice. 'What bad luck? You'll have to be extra careful at the ball, otherwise you'll end up getting covered in punch!'

'I shall not be going to the ball,' said Cicely decidedly.

Alice looked astonished. 'No? Oh, but Cicely—'

'No, Alice. It's more than I can bear. To see him walking round the Manor as though he owns the place—to have to remind myself that he does own the place—will be too terrible for me. I have told him I cannot go.'

Alice's face fell. 'Of course,' she said loyally. 'I hadn't thought of it like that. Well, who wants to go to a ball anyway?'

Cicely smiled, touched by Alice's loyalty. 'I said that I'm not going to the ball: I didn't say that you couldn't go.'

'I'm not going if you're not. They are always dull, these occasions. Always the same old people. We will stay at home instea—'

She broke off as the doorbell sounded, and a minute later another visitor was shown into the room. It was Mrs Murgatroyd.

Mrs Murgatroyd was an alarming-looking matron of five-and-forty years. Her Amazon-like figure was made even more impressive by rigid corsets, sweeping skirts and an enormous hat. But beneath her statuesque figure and her organizing nature lay a woman who never refused help to those in need, and who readily took up cudgels for those too weak to help themselves.

'Miss Haringay. I am so glad to have found you at home. Oh, Miss Babbage, I didn't realize you were here as well.'

'We were just talking about our invitations to the Manor and deciding we would not go,' said Alice.

'Quite right, too,' said Mrs Murgatroyd, drawing herself up to her full, impressive height. 'There is more to living in the country than buying a Manor house, and so I told him. You must do something about it, Miss Haringay. We are all relying on you. You must use your influence.'

'My influence?' asked Cicely. As usual, Mrs Murgatroyd had launched into the subject without preamble, expecting Cicely and Alice to know what she was talking about.

'As a Haringay,' said Mrs Murgatroyd, nodding forcefully.

'I can't stop him holding a ball if he wants to,' said Cicely, trying to follow Mrs Murgatroyd's conversation: a difficult thing, as she could not read Mrs Murgatroyd's mind.

'Not the ball,' said Mrs Murgatroyd roundly. 'The picnic.' She set herself down on the sofa and folded her arms over her capacious chest.

'The picnic?' asked Cicely.

'Yes, Cicely. The picnic.'

'Are we talking about the Sunday school picnic?' asked Cicely, hazarding a guess.

'What else? I went to tell Mr Evington about it yesterday and he told me he had no intention of letting the children hold their picnic on his lawns.'

'But it's always been held at the Manor!' cried Cicely.

'Exactly what I said.'

'And?' asked Cicely.

'And,' said Mrs Murgatroyd, with heavy emphasis, 'he looked at me as though I was the world's worst busybody and told me it would not be convenient.'

'This is too bad,' said Cicely with a frown. 'I must confess, when I sold the Manor, it never occurred to me that the new owner might not want it to be used for village events. I just assumed they would understand.'

'Well, Miss Haringay, what are you going to do?'

'I'm not sure . . .' Cicely had been about to say that she was not sure there was anything she *could* do—particularly as she did not want to visit the Manor now that it was no longer her home, as such a visit would prove painful for her—when the thought of all the children who would be disappointed if the picnic was not held at the Manor stirred her spirit. 'You're right, Mrs Murgatroyd, I must do something. I must make Mr Evington realize that he bought the lord of the Manor's responsibilities along with the Manor.' She thought of his mocking smile. Her spirit

47

wavered a little.

'Ah! That's the idea,' said Mrs Murgatroyd.

Cicely felt her resolve strengthen. Raising her chin, she said, 'In fact, I will go this very afternoon.'

CHAPTER THREE

Cicely dressed herself for the third time since luncheon. She had tried on two outfits already, but neither of them had looked smart enough. If she was going to see Mr Evington at the Manor then she needed to be looking her best. So far, he had seen her wet and bedraggled in the village pond, and wearing her shabbiest clothes as she had been attending to the range—to say nothing of seeing her with a smut on her cheek—but this afternoon she was determined that he would see her looking flawless. She had accepted the offer of Mrs Murgatroyd's maid for the afternoon, and Molly had laced her into a borrowed corset to give her figure a fashionable S-shape. Rejecting the extremes adopted by some young ladies, who, in Cicely's view, had porridge for brains, she had settled for a light lacing that enhanced her figure rather than torturing it, and allowed her to move and sit down with ease. She did not want Mr Evington to think he was talking to a stiff puppet, but to a reasonable young lady whose ideas made sound common sense.

Over her camisole, drawers and corset she put on two petticoats. The first was a plain waist petticoat and the second was trimmed with six rows of lace, frilled from the knee downwards. Then she put on her blouse—a delightful garment with a high collar and long sleeves, decorated with pin tucks down the front and a trim of lace at the yoke—before stepping into her long blue skirt, which was adorned at the hem with silk braid and lace. Once settled over the petticoats it stood out at the bottom, taking on the fashionable bell shape.

'Shall I do your hair, miss?' asked Molly.

'Yes, please,' said Cicely. She sat down so that Molly could reach her fair tresses.

Although Cicely had become adept at arranging her own hair into a pompadour style over the last few years, with the hair swept back from her face and then pinned over pads to give it its distinctive roll, she had to admit that Molly arranged it far better than she could ever do. There were no loose tendrils when Molly arranged it as there were when she did it herself, and no hint of unevenness in the shape. Then, too, with Molly arranging her hair, she could indulge in a more elaborate style. This afternoon, whilst most of her hair was piled on top of her head, one long swathe was left loose, falling down the side of her face and spilling across her blouse.

All in all, as she slipped into her bolero jacket, pinned her feathered hat on to her hair and picked up her lace-trimmed parasol, she felt ready to face a dozen Mr Evingtons. Let him laugh at her this time if he dared!

And then she was ready to go.

'Mrs Murgatroyd says I'm to stay and help you undress again, if you wish it,' said Molly.

'Oh, yes please, Molly,' said Cicely. 'That would be very kind.'

'You look lovely, miss,' said Molly, forgetting her place for a moment. 'Mr Evington won't be able to say no to you, I'm sure.'

Thanking Molly for this vote of confidence—which she had the uncomfortable feeling she would need!—Cicely set out.

The day was fine, and the walk was pleasant. Turning right out of the Lodge gates she headed up the drive, walking between the sweeping lawns that had been her mother's pride and joy. It cost her more than one pang to approach the Manor, not as its owner, but as a visitor—it was less than a week since she had moved into the Lodge, and it was still too soon for her to feel that she really belonged there, as a part of her foolishly still felt she belonged at the Manor—but determinedly she put that part of her aside. She concentrated instead on the freshness of the air, which was rich with the scent of new-mown grass, and the sky, which was full of the trilling of birdsong. It was just the sort of day that made her feel good to be alive.

If only she did not have to spoil it all by calling on Mr Evington . . .

Still, it must be done, so the sooner she got it over with the better.

Reaching the end of the drive she crossed the turning circle. Mounting the stone steps to the front door she lifted her long skirt elegantly with one hand so that she would not trip over it, and then rang the bell. It was answered promptly by a smart butler, who took her parasol, and Cicely was shown into the drawing-room, where she had a chance to look round before Mr Evington joined her.

The room, she was relieved to see, was unchanged. Although Mr Evington had only been there a day, she had dreaded to find that all the good furniture would have been pushed aside and vulgar new pieces put in its place. But so far, at least, the grand old furniture she had been forced to sell along with the Manor was still there: an elegant damasked sofa, now, alas, rather moth-eaten, which had been bought by her great-grandmother; a fine pianoforte purchased by her grandfather; a variety of occasional tables; a chaise-longue; and a few good chairs.

The door opened and she turned round swiftly to see Mr Evington enter the room.

She could not help but notice his look of

51

admiration as his eyes swept over her and she felt relieved. It had been worth it, then, the time and effort she had spent on her appearance. At least this afternoon he would have no cause for mirth.

'Miss Haringay,' he said. 'To what do I owe this pleasure?'

'You will not think it a pleasure, I fear, when I tell you why I have come,' she returned.

'No?'

'No.'

He indicated the sofa. 'Won't you sit down?'

'Thank you.'

She settled herself gracefully on the sofa. He sat down opposite her on a hard-backed chair.

'Mr Evington, I will come straight to the point.' If this was to be a business meeting she would conduct it in a business-like manner, she told herself. 'I understand that you have refused the Sunday school permission to hold their picnic at the Manor this year.'

His eyes hardened. 'Mrs Murgatroyd didn't lose any time, then,' he said under his breath. Aloud he said, 'This is a private house, Miss Haringay, it is not a venue for local jaunts.'

'That is just where you are wrong.' She returned his look with one which was equally firm. 'This is not a private house, it is a manor house, and it comes with obligations attached. You might not have heard of it, but there is such a thing as *noblesse oblige*—'

'Nobility imposes obligations,' he translated. 'You see, I am not completely ignorant, Miss Haringay—even though I am a cit,' he returned, and although there was a hint of humour in his voice, the humour did not reach his eyes. 'But I was not aware that I was a member of the nobility. Or you either,' he added sardonically.

'Nevertheless, as the owner of Oakleigh Manor you have certain obligations, and one of them is to host the Sunday school picnic,' said Cicely, raising her chin.

'And if I don't want a parcel of children running over the lawns?' he asked innocently.

'Then you tell yourself you shouldn't be so selfish and host the picnic anyway,' she returned.

His face darkened and she could tell she had hit a nerve.

'This is too much,' he said angrily. 'Lessons in selfishness from—'

'Someone who has had everything falling into her lap from the day of her birth?' she asked innocently, remembering his words to her earlier in the day. 'Yes, Mr Evington. Exactly that. The Haringays have hosted the village activities here from time immemorial, whether they have wanted to or not, and the villagers all expect you to do the same.'

He looked annoyed, and a scowl crossed his face.

'I can't see what you have against the idea,'

she said reasonably. 'Is it really so difficult for you to put the children of the village before yourself for one afternoon a year?'

'You are adept at putting other people in the wrong.' There was a note in his voice that told her he was not pleased, and there was a hard glint in his eyes. She had never noticed it before, but they darkened most attractively when he was angry, becoming almost black.

'I am adept at putting other people in the wrong when they are in the wrong,' she returned.

His brows drew together and he looked as though he would like to say something rude, but was restraining himself.

'Please don't refrain,' she said, nettled at his expression.

'From what?' he demanded, pushing himself out of his chair and striding across to the marble fireplace, where he turned and looked down at her from beneath beetling brows.

'From saying what you are thinking. Something along the lines of "If there's one thing I can't abide it's a managing female" if your expression is anything to go by,' she said with asperity.

To her surprise, instead of replying angrily, he laughed.

'Miss Haringay, sometimes it doesn't pay to be so perceptive,' he said with a wicked gleam of humour in his eye.

She smiled, and then laughed in her turn.

The atmosphere had lightened, and for the first time since she had entered the house she felt she could perhaps relax a little.

'Come now, Mr Evington, won't you host the picnic?' she asked him.

He sat down opposite her, this time on a beautiful chaise-longue, and Cicely could tell by his casual attitude that he had relented. He stretched one arm along its back and said, 'I might be persuaded to do so.'

Cicely smiled. It had not been so bad, then. In fact, it had been easy. 'Good. Then I will tell Mrs Murgatroyd—'

'On one condition.'

Cicely stiffened. 'Condition?'

'Yes.' He smiled wickedly. 'Condition. I told you that I was a stubborn man, Miss Haringay, and I am about to prove my point. I will let the Sunday school use the Manor lawns for their picnic—if you agree to attend my ball.'

Cicely paled. Attend the ball? Laugh and chatter in her beautiful home, knowing it no longer belonged to her family? Dance? Be gay? Whilst her feelings were quite the reverse? 'No. I don't think I could do that.'

'Why not?' he enquired, leaning forward. 'Can you not put your own feelings aside for one evening?'

There was a teasing note in his voice. It was, after all, exactly what she had told him to do: put his own feelings aside so that the picnic could go ahead. But still she did not want to go to the ball.

'I don't see why my presence is necessary,' she prevaricated.

'Don't you?' He stood up and walked over to the mantelpiece again. He took a sheaf of cards from behind the clock, then handed them to her. 'Fifteen replies to my invitations—and, I may say, very prompt replies: it seems in a village news travels fast,' he said, as she looked through them. 'Fifteen replies and fifteen refusals.'

She pursed her lips. 'And what does that have to do with anything?' she asked.

'Everyone for miles around is following your lead. You refused my invitation, and so the local dignitaries have done the same.'

'And you think if I change my mind they will then accept?'

'I'm certain of it.'

Cicely was certain of it, too. The local area was a close-knit community, and knowing that she did not feel she could attend the ball, all her friends had refused their invitations likewise.

'Come now, Miss Haringay, will it really be so bad?' he asked, his eyes lighting with a surprising warmth. 'An evening of good food, good conversation, good music and—I hope!—good company? If you snub me, no one will come to my ball and I will be dancing on my own.' The humour was back in his face and his voice, making him look unsettlingly attractive. And it made her wish—foolishly, for one unguarded moment—that he was not a cit who cared for nothing but loss and profit, and that he had not bought her beautiful home as though he was buying no more than piece of merchandise. For then, perhaps, she might have allowed herself to like him.

'Not on your own, surely,' she protested. 'You will have friends coming down from London.'

'Yes. I have. But I would also like to get to know my neighbours. If none of them turn up it will defeat my purpose.'

Cicely did not want to attend the ball, but she realized that it would be unfriendly of her to refuse. Mr Evington was trying to fit into the neighbourhood, and it was not kind of her to stand in his way. Especially as he had agreed to hold the picnic if she attended. Even so . . .

'I am not keen on giving in to blackmail . . .' she began hesitantly.

'Blackmail?' he asked. 'Call it rather a trade. I give you something you want, and in return you agree to give me something I want.' He gave his wicked smile. 'You were right to call me a cit, Miss Haringay. Business and trade are in my blood. And now despise me for it if you dare!'

'Indeed, I dare not,' said Cicely with a smile. His talk of trading had reminded her that trading was an important aspect of village life, and she began to realize they might have more in common than she had supposed. 'Besides, cits are not the only ones who know how to trade. You will find the villagers know all about it. Mrs Murgatroyd, for example, will be happy to trade you some of her excellent elderflower wine for some of the fruit from the Oakleigh Manor hot-houses if you ask her. I know. She has been trading with me for years!'

'Elderflower wine,' he laughed. 'I must remember that. And we, Miss Haringay? Do we have a deal?'

She made up her mind. 'We do. I will attend the ball if you promise to host the Sunday school picnic. I cannot promise that everyone else will come, mind,' she cautioned him.

'You don't need to. I will take my chances.'

There was something so unsettling in his eye as it roved over her face that Cicely stood up quickly, saying, 'I believe I must be going.'

He stood up, too.

'So soon?' he asked, crossing the space between them in one stride and taking her hand in his.

Even through her glove she could feel the heat of his fingers, and she felt suddenly hot. The strange tingling started again, filling her with a strange restlessness. She tried to draw her hand away but he held it fast.

'Will you not stay for tea?'

'Thank you, no.' She made a determined effort to free her hand, and to her relief he let

58

it go—although mixed in with the relief was a strange drop in her spirits, as though some part of her had not wanted him to.

But that was nonsense. Of course she had wanted him to let her go.

The sooner she was away from Mr Alex Evington the better, she decided. He had a most unnerving effect on her, and the less she saw of him the happier she would be.

'I must be getting back to the Lodge,' she continued. 'I'm still trying to get to grips with the range.'

His eyebrows rose, as though he had not expected her to have to bother with such things as ranges—despite the tell-tale smudge he had earlier seen on her cheek. But he made no comment, saying only, 'Very well.' He rang the bell and a minute later the butler arrived.

Exchanging goodbyes with Mr Evington, Cicely retrieved her parasol and walked out of the house. Leaving Alex looking after her, an unfathomable expression on his face.

A minute later the door opened and Roddy walked in.

'Who was *that*?' asked Roddy, glancing at Cicely, who could be seen walking down the drive.

'That,' said Alex, drawing his thoughts with difficulty back to the present, 'was Miss Cicely Haringay.'

'*Miss Haringay*?' Roddy let out a low whistle as he turned his attention again to the graceful figure of Cicely, whose straight back and delectable curves held his eye. 'I thought Miss Haringay was a spinster who indulged in good works.'

And so she is . . . in a way,' said Alex, with a wry smile.

Roddy laughed. 'It's enough to make me take up good works myself, in an effort to get to know her.'

'I shouldn't, if I were you,' said Alex.

He cursed himself as soon as he had said it. There had been an unmistakable note of warning in his voice, but fortunately Roddy, engrossed with the last glimpses of Miss Haringay's retreating figure, had not noticed.

And why had it been there, that warning note? Alex asked himself. Before realizing that, in spite of the fact he deeply resented the landed classes for what they had done to his sister, he found himself devastatingly attracted to Miss Cicely Haringay.

What was it that so attracted him to her? he asked himself. He had known many beautiful women in his time, and Cicely was not beautiful, but there was something very appealing about her. Was it her hair? he wondered. It was not remarkable in either style or colour, but there was a softness about it that made him want to reach out and touch it. Or was it her eyes? They were certainly lovely, being grey and deep-set. Or was it her nose? No, that had been a little too long. Or her mouth? His face broke into a slow smile. It was certainly kissable enough . . . Or her chin? His smile faded. No, it was definitely not her chin. It was too determined for his tastes, that chin—and it reminded him that, soft and appealing as Miss Haringay might appear, she was in fact the product of a long line of the ruling classes, people who liked to have their own way.

His eyes lost their appreciative gleam and his manner became matter-of-fact.

'You'll be pleased to know that she has changed her mind about coming to the ball,' he said.

'Ah. Good.' Roddy, too, became matter-of-fact. 'Then the rest of the neighbourhood will follow suit. Which means that the ball will be well attended, and we can go ahead with our plan.'

*   *   *

Cicely was light-hearted as she strolled down the drive, her mission successfully accomplished. Not only had she managed to secure Mr Evington's promise that the picnic could go ahead, but she had also cleared the hurdle of making her first visit to the Manor as a guest. Though saddening, the experience had been bearable, and she was now secure in the knowledge that she would be able to visit it in future without having to dread the event, which, as she was to help organize the picnic, and as she had promised to attend Mr Evington's ball, was a relief.

She followed the drive for a short way but then, instead of making her way back to the Lodge, she took one of the gravel paths that snaked through the grounds and followed it until she was almost at their edge: she had promised to visit Mrs Murgatroyd and let that worthy matron know how she had got on, and the way she was taking was the quickest route. Cutting across the grass she slipped through a gap in the railings and joined the road.

She had just done so when the sound of a familiar voice rang out in greeting.

'What ho! Cicely!'

Cicely turned and smiled. Lord Chuffington, dressed in a natty outfit of narrow trousers with a sharp crease down the front, a white shirt with high starched collar, and a brightly coloured blazer, was hailing her from the other end of the lane.

'What ho!' he said again as he ambled towards her, removing his straw boater as he did so. 'Jolly day, what?'

'Very jolly,' said Cicely, smiling at his fashionable slang. Lord Chuffington—Chuff Chuff to his friends—was an amiable young man whose family lived at Parmiston Manor, the manor house in the neighbouring village.

'Going into Little Oakleigh?' he asked, smiling brightly.

'Yes.'

'Walk along with you, if you've no objection,' said Lord Chuffington, falling into step beside her. 'I say, Cicely, you're looking dashed pretty today.'

'Thank you,' smiled Cicely.

'Dashed pretty hat,' said Lord Chuffington. 'Feathers and what-not. Deuced pretty.' He gave a grin then began to hum tunelessly.

'How is your mother?' asked Cicely. She knew from long experience that when talking to Lord Chuffington it was necessary to help the conversation along a little.

'The mater? Sound as a bell,' he said, giving her another grin.

There was a silence.

And your father?' asked Cicely politely.

'The pater? Fit as a fiddle.'

Cicely kept the conversation going by talking of village matters, but Lord Chuffington seemed distracted. He hummed and hawed and at last said, 'Look here, Cicely old thing, when you're tired of this bother with the Lodge, how about coming over to Chuffington Manor and living with me?'

'Living with you?' she asked, startled.

'Yes. You know. Lord and Lady Chuffington. Just the ticket. Any number of coves wanting to ask you, of course. Just thought I'd get my oar in first. You know, early bird catches the worm and all that.'

He paused expectantly.

'So, how about it then?' he asked.

'How about what?' asked Cicely, in something of a fog.

'You and me. Read the banns. Joyful celebrations. A good time was had by all.'

'The *banns*?' asked Cicely in astonishment.

'Got to do it sometime,' said Lord Chuffington affably.

'Do what?' asked Cicely, wondering whether he could be proposing to her, but thinking that even Chuff Chuff would have made things a little clearer if that had been the case.

'Hm? Oh! Do what? Well, you know . . .'

'No, I don't know,' said Cicely in exasperation, wishing he would explain.

'Man and wife. All that sort of thing. Orange blossom. Bridesmaids.' He smiled cheerfully.

'Chuff Chuff, are you asking me to marry you?' she asked with a sigh, realizing a direct question was the only way to find out for sure.

'Looks that way,' he said.

'Oh, Chuff Chuff, it's very sweet of you but I can't marry you,' said Cicely.

'Not to worry,' he said, not in the least put out. 'Knew you wouldn't say yes first time of asking. The mater said so, and the mater knows. Keep it for later then,' he said, with an amiable smile.

'Chuff Chuff, I won't be able to marry you later either,' Cicely said, kindly but firmly.

'Pish,' said Lord Chuffington good-naturedly. 'Ladies always say that.'

'No, really, I do assure you—'

She broke off to wish old Mr Johnson a good afternoon, then continued, 'I can't possibly marry you.'

They had by now almost reached Mrs Murgatroyd's house. The door opened and Mrs Murgatroyd herself appeared, sailing out to the gate.

'Cicely, I couldn't wait,' she said, as she greeted her. 'Do tell me how you got on. Oh,' she said, noticing Lord Chuffington. 'Chuffington. What are you doing here?'

Lord Chuffington's eyes glazed over at the sight of her. Mrs Murgatroyd was a forceful woman, and she made him go weak at the knees. 'Oh, well, just . . . well, you know . . .' he said vaguely, sauntering on the spot and looking like a startled rabbit.

'Well? Are you going or are you staying?' demanded Mrs Murgatroyd, as he hovered just outside the gate.

'Oh, rather . . . that is to say . . . yes, what,' he said hopefully.

'Lord Chuffington was courteous enough to escort me to your door, but I believe he has business elsewhere,' said Cicely kindly, knowing that Chuff Chuff could not wait to get away. He had a large number of aunts, all of whom were as forceful as Mrs Murgatroyd, and most of his life was devoted to avoiding

65

them.

'Right-o,' said Lord Chuffington amiably. He smiled at Cicely and waved vaguely in her direction. 'Toodle pip!' he said, before shambling off up the road.

'Thank goodness for that,' said Mrs Murgatroyd, as she closed the gate behind him. 'I've told you a dozen times, Cicely, you really can't go walking round the village on your own. A young lady like you ought to have a chaperon. Now, why don't you hire a companion?'

Mrs Murgatroyd had raised the subject on any number of occasions. She knew that Cicely had had to sell the Manor to pay her father's debts, but she assumed that there had been a large surplus, so that she, together with everyone else in the village, thought Cicely was comfortably off. For this reason it seemed perfectly natural to her to suggest that Cicely should hire a companion.

'You know I have cousin Gertrude,' said Cicely. 'Or at least, I will have. She would have been here by now, but she has broken her leg. Until she is better I will just have to do without a chaperon. In the country it is not so terrible for me to be without one. Besides, Chuff Chuff is harmless enough.'

'That odious nickname!' shuddered Mrs Murgatroyd. 'It makes him sound like a train'. But enough of him,' she said, as the two ladies went into the house. 'Do tell me, Cicely, how did you get on with Mr Evington?'

*   *   *

An hour later, Cicely took her leave. She had told Mrs Murgatroyd all about her interview with Mr Evington and had left that lady in a happy frame of mind, working out how many sandwiches would be required at the picnic. She was now looking forward to a peaceful evening back at the Lodge. What with one thing and another, it had been an eventful day. But there was to be one last thing that disturbed her peace of mind. As she approached the Lodge, she saw something she had not seen before. Gibson was carrying a bucket of coal from the coal bunker into the house. That in itself was not an unusual sight—since Cicely had had to dispense with the services of most of the Haringay servants because of her straitened means, Gibson had had to take on many of the chores that should, by rights, have been taken on by under-servants—but it was not this that worried Cicely particularly. It was the way Gibson put down the bucket after a few paces and rubbed his back, before picking it up and carrying on again.

Gibson never stopped and rubbed his back in her presence, but once or twice of late she had suspected he had back trouble. He often moved stiffly, and was noticeably slower than he had been a year or two before. It was not right that a man of his advanced years should be carrying heavy loads and Cicely thought, not for the first time, that she must employ a boy to help him. The only problem with that idea was that she could not afford to employ a boy.

She gave a sigh. She could not for the moment see a solution. But as she turned in at the Lodge gates she knew that she must find one. And find one soon, if she was to spare Gibson any more suffering.

CHAPTER FOUR

The following morning Cicely gave her full attention to the matter of hiring a boy. It was, unfortunately, not an easy matter to resolve. She had enough money to live on, but she had nothing to spare, and she found her thoughts wandering to Lord Chuffington's proposal. If she accepted it she would be well provided for, and Gibson would be able to retire with the benefit of an annuity to look after him in his old age. But although marrying Lord Chuffington would solve her financial difficulties, and thereby solve the problem of Gibson as well, Cicely could never seriously consider such a thing. Lord Chuffington was a dear, but she did not love him. And love, for

Cicely, was the only reason for marriage.

There remained only one alternative: she would have to seek some form of part-time employment. After much thought, she decided she would seek a job as a secretary. She was bright and well organized, and she felt she ought to be able to give satisfaction in that capacity.

Having made her decision she set out on her bicycle for the neighbouring town, in order to see if there were any suitable positions being advertised: Mr Peterson's office, she knew, dealt with such things. She did not need to earn a huge amount; just enough to be able to hire a boy to help Gibson, and perhaps to provide the loyal butler with an annuity when he retired.

On reaching the town of Oakleigh, she made directly for Mr Peterson's office and, propping her bicycle up against the wall, went in.

The office was situated up a flight of stairs, above a baker's shop. The stairs were narrow and steep. At the top they gave on to a bare waiting room, with six hard chairs pushed up against one wall. A low table with an aspidistra on it was set in front of them. On the walls were posters of young men and women busily at work, all smiling cheerily as they went about their tasks.

At the far side of the room was a desk, and behind it sat a brisk young woman who asked

Cicely her business. Fortunately Cicely was not well known in the town, and the woman did not recognize her. On Cicely's explaining that she was looking for a position, the brisk young woman asked her to take a chair before disappearing into the office, and after waiting for what seemed like an interminable time Cicely was shown in to see Mr Peterson.

'And what can we do for you?' asked Mr Peterson, looking at her over the top of his spectacles. He was a dry little man, and was seated behind a large desk that seemed too big for him.

'I am looking for work as a secretary,' said Cicely. She perched on the edge of the hard chair he had indicated when she had entered the room.

'A secretary?' He looked at her again over the top of his spectacles, as if assessing her suitability for such a position and finding her wanting. 'Do you have any experience?' He asked the question perfunctorily, and his expression was not encouraging.

'Not exactly,' she admitted. 'But I helped my father—'

'I'm afraid our clients want more solid experience than that,' he said, steepling his fingers and leaning back in his chair.

Cicely felt her backbone stiffen at the patronizing note in his voice. He had obviously decided he could reject her with a few ungracious words, but he was about to find out

70

that she would not be dismissed so easily.

'You are in the habit of arranging such matters?' she asked, with a lift of her eyebrows.

'I am,' he admitted, his eyes becoming harder.

'And you have secretarial positions on your books?' she enquired politely.

He made her wait, before saying grudgingly, 'I do.'

'Then if it is not too much trouble I would like to know what they are.'

He gave a sigh and rang a bell on his desk.

'Miss Dennis, what secretarial positions do we have on our books?' he asked, as the brisk young woman walked into the office.

'I'll get the file, Mr Peterson.'

She returned with it a few minutes later and Mr Peterson opened the file on the desk in front of him. 'Thank you, Miss Dennis, that will be all.'

The brisk young woman left the room.

Mr Peterson turned over several sheets of paper, shaking his head, then glancing up at Cicely and giving the occasional tut. But then he stopped, a single sheet of paper in his hand. He looked up at Cicely and down at the paper, then said slowly, 'There is something here that might suit you, Miss . . . ?'

'Buckworth,' said Cicely.

She had decided that she would not give her real name. If word of what she was doing got

71

back to any of her friends they would be horrified. Even worse, they would rally round and help her. But much as she loved them, in this matter Cicely did not want their help. For one thing she did not want them to know just how badly off her father's death had left her, and for another, she felt it was her responsibility to provide for Gibson and no one else's. That being the case, she wanted to do it herself.

'Miss Buckworth.' Mr Peterson accepted the name she gave him. 'It is a part-time job, for three mornings a week—'

'Good,' said Cicely. 'I am particularly interested in part-time work.' It would arouse less speculation about her whereabouts if she was only gone for a few hours each day, and with luck she would not be found out.

'And enthusiasm is required more than experience.'

'It sounds interesting,' said Cicely. 'Where is it?'

'A little out of town, I'm afraid, but not too far away. It is at Oakleigh Manor.'

'Oakleigh Manor?' Cicely tried not to let her sinking sensation show in her voice. If there was one place she could not possibly work, it was Oakleigh Manor.

'Yes.' Mr Peterson looked up at her, then down at the paper again. 'Working for a Mr Evington.'

Worse and worse, thought Cicely. Of all the

bad luck, to find the only suitable job on Mr Peterson's books was that of a secretary to Mr Evington . . . the one man in the whole of England she could not possibly work for!

'In fact, if you can wait a few minutes,' went on Mr Peterson, glancing at the clock, 'you will be able to meet him.'

'Meet him?' gasped Cicely in sudden horror. Meet Mr Evington in Mr Peterson's office, and have him discover she was looking for work? No! Not at any cost. It was far too mortifying.

'Yes,' said Mr Peterson, fortunately not noticing the horror in her voice. 'He is coming in at eleven o'clock to see if the post has been filled.'

'Oh, no, that will never do,' said Cicely, springing out of her chair. 'I mean,' she continued hastily, as she saw Mr Peterson's look of surprise, 'I mean . . .' She cast around for a likely excuse. 'I mean that unfortunately I cannot wait. I hadn't realized how late it is. I'm afraid I have to—'

At that moment there was a knock at the door. Cicely started. But to her relief it was only Miss Dennis who entered the room. The relief was short-lived, however, as Miss Dennis declared, 'Mr Evington to see you, Mr Peterson.'

Cicely felt a hot blush spread over her face. It was too awful! To be confronted by Mr Evington, here, of all places! She really did seem to have the most awful luck where he was concerned.

'Ah! Good,' said Mr Peterson, rising.

Cicely put her head down in the hope that he would not recognize her, and made to slip past Miss Dennis, murmuring that she had another appointment, but it was too late. She could not slip out of the door . . . because Alex Evington was walking in!

'Mr Evington! What a pleasure to see you,' beamed Mr Peterson: he was far more fond of employers than prospective employees.

'I'm a little early,' began Mr Evington, 'but—'

'And a good thing too,' Mr Peterson interrupted him, wreathed in smiles. 'There is a young woman here, looking for a job as a secretary. She is a little reluctant to take a job at the Manor, but I am sure you can persuade her it will be just the thing. Mr Evington, may I present Miss Buckworth?'

Cicely felt her cheeks flame. As if it wasn't bad enough that Mr Evington should discover her seeking employment, he had to find her using an assumed name as well!

She tried to raise her eyes, telling herself not to be such a coward, but they remained firmly fixed on the floor.

'Miss Buck—' Mr Evington stopped mid-sentence, as he turned towards her and realized who she was. '—worth,' he finished, in a completely different tone of voice.

'Come, come, Miss Buckworth, no need to

be shy. Mr Evington will not eat you, you know,' said Mr Peterson jovially, completely misunderstanding the reason for Cicely's blushes.

With a supreme effort Cicely raised her head.

'I dare say Miss Buckworth feels the Manor is too isolated a place for her to work in, being so far out in the country. As I believe I explained to you when you asked us to find you someone, Mr Evington, most young people prefer to be closer to town, where there is a bit more life. But I'm sure you will be able to convince her otherwise,' declared Mr Peterson.

'No, no, I do assure you, Mr Evington cannot,' said Cicely, wishing the ground would open up and swallow her. Realizing that it was not likely to do anything so obliging, however, she made to hurry away.

Except Mr Evington was blocking the doorway.

Cicely swallowed, hoping fervently that he would move.

Mr Evington turned to Mr Peterson. 'If we could have a moment alone,' he said smoothly.

'But of course,' said Mr Peterson, with an ingratiating smile.

A moment later he had left them, and Cicely was face to face with Alex Evington, and again in the most mortifying circumstances. She seemed to be cursed! First

75

he saw her fall in the duck pond, then he saw her with a smut on her face, and now he found her seeking work under an assumed name.

'Mr Peterson is mistaken, I assure you,' said Cicely, trying her best to hide her agitation, and determined to convince Mr Evington that she was not looking for work. 'I have no need to supplement my income and I am not in the least desirous of becoming a secretary.'

The words were clumsy and out of her mouth before she had given any thought to them, and she was convinced he could not fail to see through them. Indeed, he seemed to realize she was lying, because something in his face changed. His eyes, which had been astonished, now hardened . . . but when he spoke, Cicely was surprised to discover that he had misunderstood her words and her manner entirely.

'You mean you have not the least desire to become *my* secretary,' he said bitingly. There was an air of tension about him, and she was forcibly reminded of the fact that his background was very different to hers. If he had been a country gentleman he would not have made such a remark, nor would he have spoken so bitingly. But Alex Evington was completely different from the men she was used to. He was harder, more ruthless, and disinclined to sweep anything under the carpet. It made things far more difficult for her. And yet in a way she respected him for it.

'That is not what I meant at all,' she said, raising her head. Now that the encounter could not be avoided she knew she must rise to the challenge, and she prepared to defend herself against his mistaken beliefs. But it was not going to be easy.

'Isn't it?' he demanded.

His eyes darkened with some barely suppressed emotion which was clearly composed of anger, but there was something else there as well. Something it was much more difficult to read.

'You are clearly bored with doing nothing all day long,' he continued, 'or else why would you visit such an office? And as you told Mr Peterson you wanted to find a position as a secretary—unless you are calling him a liar?' he digressed, his voice hard.

'Certainly not,' she replied, her own anger beginning to rise.

'Very well, then. As you told Mr Peterson you wanted to find a position as a secretary, I may safely assume that a position as a secretary is what you were looking for. But the second you were offered one at Oakleigh Manor you changed your mind. And as soon as I entered the room you decided you must leave.'

Cicely felt a feeling of frustration wash over her. He had got it all wrong. But how could she tell him so without confessing that she needed money? Which she had no intention of doing. Her pride simply would not let her.

'I know you don't like me, Miss Haringay,' he went on harshly, 'but is it really necessary to make it so obvious every time we meet?'

By this time Cicely had recovered somewhat from her shock, and the injustice of this last remark stung her. 'I hardly think you are in a position to lecture me on my behaviour,' she returned. 'Your own behaviour is hardly a model of decorum.' Gaining confidence, she raised her chin and looked him in the eye. 'You delight in laughing at me every time we meet, and when you are not laughing at me you are making it clear what you think of the landed classes. Can you really say you would have employed me, even if I had applied for the post?'

'I—' He broke off.

'There. You see. You don't like me any more than I like you,' she retorted. 'We can both of us congratulate ourselves on having had a lucky escape. And that being the case I will bid you good day.'

She turned towards the door, but he surprised her by saying, 'Yes. I would.'

'I beg your pardon?' she asked, turning round.

'You're right.' His mouth was grim. 'I don't like you any more than you like me, but I would still have offered you the post, because you are the one person in all the country who would be able to give me exactly what I need.'

'Oh? And what is that?' she demanded, wanting to maintain her anger, because anger made it easier for her to deal with him, but intrigued despite herself.

He ran his hand through his dark hair. 'An intimate knowledge of the local people and the customs of the Manor. It isn't only the Sunday school picnic.' He shook his head, as though bewildered. 'It's everything else. The Manor seems to be the hub of the village and everyone seems to be looking to me as the owner to carry on all the traditions. But I have no idea what they are. You, however, *do* know. I thought at first I could simply declare that the Manor was a private house and have done with it, but you're right, I can't. Not if I want to be accepted here. Which means I need someone to help me. And the only way of finding someone seemed to be to advertise. But the candidates I've seen so far know less about running a Manor than I do. Not the day-to-day running, of course, but making it work as a part of village life.'

Cicely wavered. The job he was outlining was tempting. Even so, working for Mr Evington . . . no, it did not bear thinking about. It was not just that she resented him for having bought the Manor, and having bought it without even bothering to look at it, and it was not just the way he laughed at her almost every time they met. Nor was it the fact that she did not like cits, who came into the country with their noise and their pollution and their flashy way of living, making themselves a nuisance to everybody else. No. It was because of the way his eyes flashed when he smiled, and the way it made her feel. Why it should make her feel that way—why indeed it should make her feel anything—she did not know, but she did not want the feeling. It made matters too confusing. Mr Evington as a bad-mannered cit whom she disliked because he had bought her lovely home she could cope with. Mr Evington who had a sense of the ridiculous and a lively sense of humour—attributes which, in normal circumstances, Cicely both enjoyed and shared—and whose eyes flashed wickedly when he smiled, was something else.

To say nothing of the way he made her feel when he touched her. He seemed to have the power to turn her world upside down and she was not sure she liked the feeling: it made her feel vulnerable, out of control.

'And then there is the inventory,' he said, thrusting his hands deep in his trouser pockets. 'I mean to catalogue the contents of the Manor,' he explained. 'As I bought it partly furnished I would like to know exactly what there is, in case anything goes missing, or there is ever a fire, and to do so I need a full inventory. And who better than you to help me make one? You know the house and its contents better than anyone else—if you could put your dislike of me aside enough to come and work for me, that is.'

She wavered even more. On the one hand, she thought the task of making an inventory of the Manor might be a sad one for her, as her beautiful family heirlooms belonged to her no more, but on the other hand she could not bear the thought of a stranger doing it. At least if she made the inventory she would be able to treat the house and its contents with the love and respect they deserved.

'Well, Miss Haringay? Will you accept the post?'

Cicely hesitated for a minute, but the job appealed to her and besides, without any qualifications or experience she knew that it was the only offer of employment she was likely to receive. 'I . . .' she said, before asking herself if she was being wise. But wise or not it was the only way forward. 'I will.'

'A truce, then?' he asked, his eyes warming.

He really had the most attractive eyes when he looked at her just so, she thought. And for some reason they sent shivers coursing through her entire body . . .

'At least until you have told me what is expected of me as the owner of the Manor, and helped me to make an inventory of the contents?' he continued.

She took a deep breath and then nodded. 'A truce.'

He smiled and held out his hand for her to shake.

Cicely quavered. She was forcibly reminded of the effect it had had on her when he had taken her hand at the Manor. It had set her pulse racing and filled her stomach with the strangest tinglings. And yet she could not see any way of avoiding it.

She took a deep breath, and then put her hand into his.

As his strong fingers closed around her own, she felt a surge of energy course through her, making her tingle from head to toe. It was a good thing she was wearing gloves, she thought with a gasp, for if he had closed his fingers around her bare hand the sensation would have been overwhelming.

Hastily, she retrieved her hand. Or tried to. But he held on to it, his eyes locked on to her own.

'When . . .' She swallowed. For some reason she had difficulty getting her words out. Her heart was beating rapidly, and her voice was little more than a breathless gasp. 'When would you like me to start?'

'On Monday, if that is convenient,' he said. His eyes still held her own.

It wasn't just the way they flashed that attracted her. It was their dark depths that fascinated her.

'Very well.' She tried to withdraw her hand again, and this time he allowed her to do so. She took a deep breath to steady herself. 'Until Monday, then.'

She moved to go past him. For a minute he blocked her way. Then he moved aside and allowed her to walk out of the office.

She was trembling from head to foot as she descended the stairs. She had just agreed to become Alex Evington's secretary, and she had the alarming feeling that she had been foolish. To be close to Mr Evington three times a week would be difficult, as he was, without doubt, the most provoking man she had ever met. And yet despite this, being with him made her pulse beat more quickly and produced the most pleasurable sensations inside her.

How would she fare, alone with him at the Manor? she wondered. Would she be able to concentrate on her duties?

She lifted her chin. She must. She needed the money. She would just have to curb her feelings for Mr Evington, whatever they might be—for they seemed to be a confused and confusing mass of conflicting emotions—and concentrate on being an efficient secretary instead.

And having made this resolution she reclaimed her bicycle and set off back to the Lodge.

*   *   *

'You've taken a position as Mr Evington's secretary?' asked Alice in astonishment the following day, as the two young women tidied the garden at the Lodge.

'I have.' Cicely pulled the dead heads from the blossoming plants and took them over to the small compost heap behind the house.

'I didn't know you were so short of money,' said Alice, her astonishment giving way to a frown.

'I didn't want you to know,' admitted Cicely. 'In fact, I wasn't going to tell you about my job. But as I will be at the Manor for three mornings every week from now on I felt I had to tell you. It would be just too difficult to keep thinking up excuses as to why I was never at home.'

'I should think so, too,' said Alice.

'But I don't want anyone else to know. Everyone thinks the sale of the Manor left me well provided for and I don't want them to think any differently. I may not have much money but I still have my pride.'

Alice nodded. 'Your secret's safe with me. And as I am the only one who visits you regularly in the mornings, no one else need suspect anything. Unless they see you at the Manor?'

'It isn't likely. And if they do, well, why shouldn't I be there? With the Sunday school picnic coming up, and after it a variety of activities which involve the Manor, they will simply think I am talking Mr Evington into behaving as the owner of the Manor should.'

'You must have softened towards him, then,'

said Alice, as she began to weed the rose bed. 'For you to take a job with him, I mean. A few days ago you could not even bear to hear his name mentioned.' She sat back on her heels. 'I think it's a good thing. The village is too small a place for people to take a dislike to one another.'

'I dislike Mr Evington as much as I ever did, and he feels the same way about me,' said Cicely decidedly. 'We have, however, discovered we need each other and we have decided to call a truce.'

Alice gave her a sideways look.

'There is no need to look like that,' said Cicely vigorously. 'When I say we have discovered we need each other I mean we need each other's help. Mr Evington needs someone to show him the ropes at the Manor, and I need a job. Fortunately he thinks I need one because I am bored, rather than realizing I need one so that I can earn some money and then hire a boy to help Gibson. If he knew how straitened my circumstances were it would be just too mortifying. And so we have come to an arrangement which suits us both.'

'You haven't changed your mind about him now that you've come to know him a little?' asked Alice.

'No. In fact, quite the opposite. Granted, he has a certain charm'—and the most wickedly attractive eyes, she thought, but did not say so; together with having had the most startling effect on her every time he touched her—'but he is still a brash businessman who is out of place in Little Oakleigh.'

'Well, his brashness is not to be wondered at,' said Alice thoughtfully. 'Mrs Sealyham has a cousin who has a friend who knows all about Mr Evington. He has only recently made his money by clever dealings in the city, but before that he was working as a Liverpool dock hand.'

'A dock hand?' Cicely sat up and pushed a tendril of ash-blonde hair away from her face.

'So Mrs Sealyham's cousin's friend says,' said Alice.

'And if Mrs Sealyham's cousin's friend says it, it must be true,' Cicely joked. 'Still,' she went on thoughtfully, 'it wouldn't surprise me. When we first met he said something rather odd. On offering to help me retrieve my bike from the duck pond I told him it would make him dirty, and he said, "I've been dirtier".'

Cicely recalled his face as he had said it, and the trace of bitterness in his voice. If he had indeed worked on the docks she could at last understand it. Was that why he resented the landed classes? Because he had had to work so hard for everything he had? That was a part of it, perhaps. And yet, somehow, Cicely felt there was more to it. His dislike of the landed classes seemed more personal.

'There you are then,' said Alice. She paused, and then a minute later said, 'So you haven't changed your mind about Mr Evington at all? You still don't like him?'

'No, I don't.'

Alice sighed. 'It's a pity.' Then said, with a far-away look in her eyes, 'I think he's dreamy.'

'Dreamy?' Cicely sounded surprised.

'Come on, Cicely, you can't pretend he isn't handsome. And his eyes have the most attractive way of flashing when he smiles . . . or hadn't you noticed?'

'No,' said Cicely, digging in the flower bed with extra vigour. 'I hadn't.'

She wondered a moment later why she had lied. Because she *had* noticed the way his eyes flashed when he smiled, on many occasions, and how attractive it made him. But admitting it made her feel vulnerable. And for some unknown reason she felt it was far safer to pretend she liked nothing about him.

CHAPTER FIVE

'The Harvest Supper?' asked Alex Evington, looking at the letter in his hand.

'Yes,' said Cicely, taking it as he passed it to her. 'It's usually held here.'

It was Monday morning, and they were sitting in Mr Evington's study, going through the post. The summer sun was shining through the window, lighting up the piles of paper on

87

his desk.

'Gibson can give you some help with arranging it if you like,' she continued. 'He was the butler at the Manor for twenty years. He knows how these things are done.'

'That would be very helpful.'

'I will make a note of it in the diary,' said Cicely. 'Then you can check the date with the rector before making the final arrangements.'

He nodded, before taking up the next letter.

'Christmas carolling,' he said.

'Goodness, they're getting in early,' said Cicely, taking the letter from him. 'The carolling isn't usually arranged until much later in the year, but it's true the carol singers usually meet up at the Manor after they have been round the village—after singing a rousing selection of carols they are invited in for punch.'

'We had better write back, then, and say it can go ahead,' he said.

'Miss Fotherington's wedding breakfast,' he said, picking up the next letter.

'Miss Fotherington's wedding breakfast?' echoed Cicely in surprise.

'Yes. *Dear Mr Evington,*' said Alex, reading aloud, *'As I'm sure you're aware it has always been the custom for the owner of the Manor to provide the wedding breakfast for any young lady who marries within the parish. The Haringays have always upheld this tradition, and I am sure—'*

'Of all the cheek!' exclaimed Cicely, taking the letter out of his hand. *'The custom for the owner of the Manor to provide the wedding breakfast* indeed!'

'Does that mean it isn't?' he asked, with a wry smile.

'It most certainly is not! Mrs Fotherington is the most penny-pinching woman you could ever hope to meet—or perhaps I should say, the most penny-pinching woman you could ever hope *not* to meet—but this is outrageous, even for her. You will not answer this letter. I will answer it for you,' said Cicely firmly. *'The Haringays always upheld this tradition!* The woman takes my breath away!'

'It's a good thing I hired you,' he laughed. 'No one else would have been able to tell me that Mrs Fotherington is a fraud, and I might well have ended up paying for her daughter's wedding feast!'

'A sharp set-down is what she needs,' said Cicely, bristling at Mrs Fotherington's audacity.

He laughed. 'Then we will give her one. Well, that is all the post for today. But now, there is something else I need your help with. I've been looking for a key for the old stable block but I can't find one—if it's suitable, I mean to keep my motor there.'

'The key's in the garden room, in the top drawer of the bureau,' she said. 'But I'm not sure about using it for your motor—although,

89

of course, you must use it as you see fit,' she said, remembering with a sudden pang that she was no longer the owner of the Manor.

'Oh. And why is that? Is it already full?'

Cicely nodded. 'It houses my father's collection.'

He raised his eyebrows. 'Your father kept his collection in the *stables*?' he asked.

She nodded. 'Yes.'

'As the doors have been locked ever since I arrived, I suppose he did not collect horses?' he asked, with a teasing smile.

'No.' She smiled fondly as she remembered her father. 'Not horses. My father collected boneshaking machines.'

'Boneshak—you mean he collected bicycles?'

'Yes.' Her smile brightened. 'My father loved bicycles. He was fascinated by their workings and belonged to an inventors' club whose sole purpose was to devise more of the machines. He sat me on one before I could walk and I loved it. I have been riding ever since.' Her smile faded. 'But they will be of no interest to you, of course,' she remarked.

She was saddened. Mr Evington would no doubt want to dispose of the rickety machines so that he would have somewhere to keep his motor car.

'On the contrary.' He smiled, and she noticed again how it made his eyes light up in the most compellingly attractive way. 'I found an abandoned bicycle when I was a boy and I spent all my free time riding it. I'll look forward to seeing your father's collection.'

'It really needs cataloguing,' said Cicely, her interest awakened. 'My father intended to open a museum, so that when people came to visit the Manor they could see the various machines in his possession and chart the history of the bicycle.'

'I think that's an excellent idea. When we have finished on the inventory of the house, we can move on to the boneshakers. In fact, I suggest we go out and take a look at them now.'

'Oh, yes!' Cicely's enthusiasm was caught by the idea.

It did not take him long to find the key, and before long the two of them were walking round the Manor and heading towards the old stables which lay behind it.

'I just hope I picked up the right one,' he said, as they approached the stables.

He fit the key in the lock and turned it. The stable door swung wide.

'Shall we?'

He stood aside to let her pass, and Cicely went into the stable. It was cool and dark. There was a slightly musty background scent, but the overwhelming smell was of hay.

'It really should be cleared out,' said Cicely, looking at the soft piles of dried grass as her eyes accustomed themselves to the dim light.

Here and there pieces of dried clover could be seen sticking out of the mounds, adding to the sweet smell.

Alex nodded absently, but his attention was on the boneshakers and not on the hay.

'It's a treasure house,' he said appreciatively, as his eyes too accustomed themselves to the dim light.

Cicely was gratified at his interest. 'Do you really think so?'

He nodded. 'I do.'

Arranged lovingly in the stable were bicycles of every size and description. Some of the contraptions had one wheel, others had two or three. Some of them had wheels of the same size, and others had wheels of startlingly different sizes, most notable of which was a magnificent penny-farthing machine.

'It must have taken your father a lifetime to assemble his collection,' he said, walking amongst the machines and looking them over.

'It did,' said Cicely. 'He was always interested in boneshakers—although velocipedes, he always insisting on calling them—and began collecting them at an early age.'

'Do they work?' Alex stopped beside an odd-looking contraption.

'Oh, yes. My father rode them regularly.'

'How on earth do you ride this one?' he asked, regarding a huge wheel, some six feet in diameter, that was stored at the back of the barn. It was made of two halves which were joined round the circumference but ballooned out in the centre to provide room for a seat in between.

'I'll show you,' laughed Cicely. 'If you'll help me take it outside?'

Alex readily lent his assistance, and between them he and Cicely wheeled the strange contraption out of the old stables and into the yard.

'It's not easy with a long skirt,' said Cicely, thinking that if she had known they were likely to look at the bicycles she would have worn her divided cycling skirt, 'but I think I can show you what has to be done.'

She opened the cage-like machine at one side and climbed in, settling herself on the narrow seat. 'If you can close the wheel,' she said.

Are you sure you're going to be all right in there?'

'Quite sure. But you will need to keep out of the way. This type of machine is difficult to steer, and I won't answer for the consequences if you get in its path.'

He laughed. 'Then I'd better look lively.'

He closed the cage and stepped quickly aside as Cicely began to pedal. The huge wheel began to turn, with her inside it, the clever construction of the seat keeping her still and upright whilst the wheel rolled along in a straight line. She steered it with levers inside the machine, and felt all the exhilaration of the wind in her hair as she rode to the end of the yard.

Stopping the boneshaker was a precarious task, but she managed it with skill, and before the wheel could topple she felt Mr Evington catching hold of it, steadying it as she climbed out.

'That looks like fun,' he remarked.

'It is.'

'I think I might have a go.'

'It takes some getting used to,' she warned him.

'I'll take my chances,' he said, with a wry smile.

He climbed into the machine and Cicely closed it round him, then he began pedalling and soon he too was bowling along. When it came to stopping the machine, however, he wobbled precariously and only just managed to save himself from disaster.

'I think I'll try something a little more conventional this time,' he said, going back into the stables and wheeling out a cycle with two wheels of almost the same size. He climbed on and began riding round the yard.

'Be careful,' called Cicely warningly, as he began to build up speed, suddenly remembering that that particular boneshaker had not been in a good state of repair. 'The brakes don't—'

But her warning came too late. Heading for the horse trough he lost control of the steering, and tried to apply the brakes. They did not work, and a minute later he was thrown into the water!

Cicely could not help it. She doubled up with mirth.

He sat up, leaning back on his arms, with his knees pulled up in front of him. His jacket and trousers were drenched. Water dripped from his hair, which was black and sleek, revealing the contours of his head. 'It isn't funny,' he said, annoyed, as he pushed himself out of the trough, dripping wet.

'Oh, but it is!' gasped Cicely as she clutched her sides. 'Turnabout's fair play!' she said, remembering the way he had laughed at her when she had fallen in the duck pond. But then her expression changed, for he began walking towards her with the most determined air, and a wicked smile on his face. 'Oh!' She let out a startled gasp, as she saw him stretch out his dripping wet hands in front of him. 'Oh, no!' she exclaimed, still laughing, and then turned and ran back into the stables. She knew exactly what he meant to do. He meant to shake himself all over her to pay her back for laughing at him!

She glanced back over her shoulder, hoping he had given up the pursuit, but on the contrary he was now running after her, and he was gaining!

She sprinted into the stables, but it was too late. He took her arm, halting her flight, but

95

she was determined she would not be caught so easily. Trying to shake off his hand she half turned, and tripped on her skirt. She balanced for a moment, but then gravity took effect and she fell back into the sweet-smelling hay—and Mr Evington, trying to prevent her from falling, was caught off balance and tumbled after her.

And then everything changed. Because somehow he had ended up on top of her.

Cicely's heart missed a beat.

And then it resumed its course, as she was aware of his body pressing down on her. It was intoxicating. As his weight pinned her to the hay, pressing her deeper into the yielding pile, she gasped.

As if in answer he shifted on top of her, taking his weight on his arms and lifting his body so that it was barely grazing her own. But if anything that made things worse. Shivers of awareness shot through her, and her body felt more vibrant than it had ever felt in her life. Every one of her nerves was on fire. The sensation exhilarated and alarmed her, even as shivers washed over her, thrilling through her entire body from head to foot.

For one heady moment she forgot to breathe.

Only to start again with a low moan as his hand drifted over her cheek, caressing her with a touch that left her feeling weak.

As his fingers grazed her cheekbone she felt

herself yearning for him, although in what way she was yearning she did not know. All she knew was that she wanted to be even closer to him. She revelled in the firm touch of his fingers as they traced the line of her jaw and again caressed her smooth cheeks.

She began to breathe more rapidly as his eyes followed his fingers, trailing over her face before finally coming to rest on her lips. And then his face lowered towards hers. It was so close that she could see the rough stubble that covered his chin. It was intensely masculine, the dark shadow drawing her eyes and focusing them on his mouth. His lips moved closer still, so close that she could feel the heat of his breath. Her own parted unknowingly and her eyes began to close.

He kissed her eyelids, then brushed her brow with gossamer-light kisses before trailing his mouth across her cheek towards her parting lips.

She waited in an ecstasy of suspense for his mouth to meet hers, and—

'Alex!' The cry broke the silence.

But not the spell that held them. It barely scratched the surface.

'Alex!' It came again.

Cicely stirred.

Alex began to pull away from her, and she felt a surge of almost unbearable frustration; opening her eyes she saw a matching emotion sweep over his face. His eyes lingered for one long, hot moment on her lips, and then, with a supreme effort of will, he pushed himself up.

'Alex! Where are you?' The cry came from the direction of the house.

With one last, longing look at Cicely, Alex rose to his feet.

Shakily, Cicely followed, gradually breaking free of the spell that had gripped her and suddenly overcome with the enormity of what had just happened. She felt herself flushing to the roots of her hair as she realized she had almost succumbed to his masculinity, his warm, earthy scent, and his hypnotic charm.

She took a few moments to steady herself. She looked down and realized that she was covered in tell-tale pieces of hay. With trembling fingers she picked them from her long mauve skirt and her white blouse, before following Alex out of the dimly lit barn into the sunshine.

Fortunately, the owner of the voice that had brought them to their senses was not in sight. Still, she was badly shaken by what had just occurred and she had an overwhelming urge to hide from her unruly feelings by running away.

'I . . . I should be going,' she said. She did not know what time it was and therefore did not know if it was time for her to go home, but she did not care. She could not possibly stay after what had happened.

'Cicely . . .'

'Miss Haringay,' she said in a sudden panic.

98

She could not possibly respond to the throatiness of his voice, which sent new thrills coursing through her body. She must suppress such feelings at all cost.

Some of the molten heat left his eyes, as though her formal manner had reminded him of the true relationship between them, that of employer and employee.

'Of course,' he said formally, his voice rigidly controlled. 'And I must go and change.' He turned, as though he was about to go, and then said, 'I hope this will not affect our working relationship.' He hesitated. 'You need not be afraid of me. There will be no more . . . horseplay . . . in future, I assure you.' He made an attempt at lightness. 'One ducking in the trough is quite enough!'

She appreciated his attempt to take the tension out of the situation by making a joke of it, and she gave a weak smile in return, doing what she could to help him pass off the awkward circumstance. 'I am sure it is.'

'I will see you on Wednesday as arranged?' he asked.

She took a deep breath, then nodded. 'You will.'

'Good. Then I will bid you goodbye—until Wednesday.'

'Until Wednesday,' she said.

He strode off towards the Manor.

As she watched him go, a part of Cicely felt she never wanted to see Alex Evington again.

He was too unsettling, and the effect he had on her was too disturbing. But another part of her longed to be with him, to feel his strong fingers tracing the line of her jaw and caressing the curve of her cheek, and to see his eyes, hot with desire, piercing her own.

Oh! It had been heavenly.

But it must not be allowed to happen again. She knew very little about Alex Evington, but everything she knew told her that she must not fall victim to his undoubted charm. She would have to carry on seeing him again, unfortunately, because she must carry on with her job as his secretary if she wanted to be able to employ a boy to help Gibson, but she meant to be on her guard. She found that she believed him when he said there would be no more horseplay—from the look on his face when he had heard the cry that had jolted them both back to reality, she had no doubt that he did not want something so inappropriate to happen again—but even so, she knew she would have to treat him with more than the usual distance if she was to prevent her unruly feelings from rising to the surface.

Resettling her straw hat on her head, she made an effort to compose herself, then retreated to the safety of the Lodge, where she hoped to forget all about Alex Evington. But even as she thought it, she knew the hope was vain.

* * *

Alex cursed himself as he strode back to the Manor, his clothes dripping wet. What on earth had he been thinking of, chasing Miss Haringay like that? He had had a warning of the effect she had on him when he had shaken her hand in Mr Peterson's office, and he should have been on his guard. Instead of which he had behaved like a green boy, careering round on a bicycle and plunging into the horse trough, and then giving in to an urge to pay her back for laughing at him by making her as wet as he was. If he had been sensible he would have done nothing of the kind. He would have excused himself and returned to the Manor to change his clothes, and no harm would have been done. But had he done it? No. He had chased her into the stables, and when she had tripped on her skirt he had not been able to hold her upright but had instead tumbled on top of her, unleashing the chemistry that existed between them.

He felt again the raw sensations that had gripped him when he had fallen on top of her. Her soft flesh yielding beneath him had sent an electrical charge through him that had been stronger and more powerful than anything he had ever felt before, and despite all his experience he had been taken aback by its sheer force.

Even now, he could hardly believe its intensity. He had experienced chemical attraction before, but never on that scale. It had been so overwhelming that he had almost given into it and kissed her where she had fallen in the warm, fragrant hay.

And more than kissed her . . .

As he thought again of her soft hair, deep-set eyes and beautiful lips he felt his body stir. She had looked so right beneath him that he had felt that was where she was meant to be. He had been so overwhelmed by the feeling that it had taken all of his self control to stop him making love to her. But even then, he had not been able to prevent himself taking her face in his hands and running his fingers over her smooth and delicate skin. He remembered the soft silkiness of it beneath his fingers, and remembered how it had made him long to run his hands over her entire body. Damn the current fashions! he thought, as he remembered the way her clothes covered her from her chin to her toes—although it was probably fortunate that they did. If they had left any more of her uncovered, he doubted if he would have been able to stop himself from running his hands over every naked inch.

He made an effort to turn his thoughts into different channels. He loosened his tie as he strode towards the house—for some reason the damn thing felt far too tight—glad of the cold water that had drenched him, as it went some way towards cooling the passionate flames that still gripped him, even now Cicely had gone.

Still, there was one bright side to the situation, he thought. At least he had managed to stop himself. He had Roddy to thank for that. The sound of his brother's voice had recalled him to reality just in time, for it would have been madness to have given in to the urges that had overtaken him and made him their plaything in the barn. To even think of kissing Cicely Haringay had been pure insanity. Cicely Haringay, of all people, who looked down on him and regarded him with contempt! If he had had to experience an attraction so strongly, why could it not have been for a nice young woman who was fun to be with, instead of one of the landed gentry who had been born with a silver spoon in her mouth.

But Cicely is fun to be with.

The unwelcome thought pushed itself into his mind.

How else would he have been able to forget himself and behave like a boy, careering round the stable yard on a boneshaking machine, if she had not been fun? He did not want to face the fact, but he had not enjoyed himself so much in years. He had had the responsibilities of a man put on his shoulders at an early age. With a dead father and a sickly mother he had become the man of the household at the age of

103

twelve and had done what he could to provide for the family. He had taken any job that had offered, and had worked long hours so that Roddy could get the necessary schooling to take up a white-collar job. He had found Katie a place in service, and then, having done what he could for his brother and sister, he had set about making his fortune. And when he had made it he had rescued Katie from service and Roddy from the life of a pettifogging clerk. It had been work, work, work. Not that he resented any of it. He had done well and he had helped his family, and he was proud of that fact. But there had not been much time for anything else.

And then, out of the blue, he had found himself having fun with Miss Cicely Haringay. She might have been born with a silver spoon in her mouth, but she was lively and intelligent and, contrary to what he had at first supposed, she had a sense of humour. No matter how difficult it was, he had to acknowledge that her company had given him very real enjoyment. Her knowledge had proved invaluable, and her daring in riding the bone shaking machines had proved impressive. The love she had obviously borne her father had made him admire her—loyalty was important to him, and it was clear Miss Haringay knew the meaning of it—and her laughter when he had fallen in the horse trough had proved she had a sense of the ridiculous that was every well bit as developed as his own.

But she was still a Haringay. Still from a long line of landowners who thought that ordinary people were beneath them. Still the kind of person who would have dismissed Katie for something she didn't do.

The thought sobered him.

Yes, Cicely came from a different world, and he would do well to remember it.

He turned the corner of the stable yard and almost bumped into Roddy coming in search of him.

'There you are!' said Roddy, before stopping and looking at him in amazement. His face broke into a grin. 'What happened to you?'

'Don't ask,' said Alex in exasperation.

Roddy laughed. 'Fell in a duck pond?' he enquired, humorously.

Alex laughed, too. 'If you must know, I fell in the horse trough.'

'The horse trough! What on earth were you doing falling in the horse trough?'

'I was riding a boneshaker and the brakes didn't work. It pitched me off, head first.'

'That explains it!' said Roddy, taking in Alex's suit, the straight trousers and well-cut jacket dripping with water and covered with pieces of hay. 'Or at least, it explains why you're so wet. But why are you covered in dried grass?'

Alex brushed the hay off his jacket. 'It's a

long story,' he said. Adding to himself, and not one I intend to divulge.

'It's a good thing Miss Haringay didn't see you, otherwise she would have been able to get her own back on you for laughing at her when she fell in the duck pond!' laughed Roddy.

'Miss Haringay did see me,' said Alex, 'and I assure you she paid me back in full for my amusement at her own ducking!'

Roddy laughed even louder. 'Good for her!'

'And now I have to get out of these wet things—which are probably ruined,' said Alex, looking ruefully at his suit. 'What was it you wanted me for?' he asked, as the two of them returned to the Manor.

Roddy's eyes took on a bright gleam. 'I wanted to tell you the news. Our plan has worked—or, at least, the first part of it. The Honourable Martin Goss has replied to your invitation to the house-warming ball.'

Alex's eyes became alert. He stopped and faced Roddy. 'And?' he demanded.

'He thanks you for your kind invitation—and expresses himself delighted to be able to attend.'

'Hah!' Alex's eyes lit up. 'We've tempted him, Roddy. And once tempted I have no doubt we'll catch him.' His face became more thoughtful. 'Now all we have to do is make sure we have a sufficiently attractive bait.'

CHAPTER SIX

Shall I or shan't I? thought Cicely, as she prepared to go to the Manor on Wednesday morning. Shall I or shan't I wear my gloves?

Long gloves formed a part of the fashionable outfit customarily worn by young ladies, but for her job at the Manor they were hardly practical, which was why she had not worn them on the previous Monday. She could not write easily whilst wearing them, nor could she operate the typewriter. On the other hand, they would protect her from any more electrical sensations if she should accidentally come into contact with Mr Evington.

The effect he had had on her still shocked her. She had never reacted like that to a man before. On occasion she had touched other gentlemen, but even when not wearing gloves she had felt nothing untoward—not even a spark. And what she had felt when touching Mr Evington had definitely been much more than a spark. It had been like a sheet of lightning, blasting its way from his body to hers, electrifying her from head to foot.

She was still not sure if she had liked the sensation. On the one hand it had been utterly wonderful, but on the other, it had been alarming because, like lightning, it had been completely beyond her control.

She had tried to put all thoughts of what had happened in the barn out of her mind, but she had been unable to do so. It had been so consuming that she had not been able to forget it. Indeed, she had spent most of the last two days thinking about it, although she had tried determinedly to think of something—anything—else. But the memory would not go away.

It was not just that Mr Evington had almost kissed her, it was that she had wanted him to.

That fact had disturbed her more than any other. She had tried to deny it, but could not. When he had stroked his fingers across her face she had wanted him to cover her lips with his own.

Such a thought was too agitating for her to dwell on. She picked up her long gloves, once again trying to drive such thoughts from her mind. If she wore her gloves then any sparks would be muted—but it would be extremely difficult to do her job. She could not fulfil her tasks as a secretary whilst wearing gloves.

No, she decided at last, putting her gloves back on her dressing-table, she could not wear them. But she would take care she did not touch Mr Evington again.

Fortunately, he seemed to have the same idea, for when she joined him at the Manor half an hour later, he sat determinedly on the opposite side of his desk and adopted a coolly formal manner, treating her very much as a secretary and not as a young woman he had nearly kissed on the sweetly scented hay. To begin with she was apprehensive and sat rigidly on the edge of her seat, ready to fly at any moment. But when she saw that he meant to avoid contact as much as she did—when she saw him laying letters on the desk instead of handing them to her, then leaving her to pick them up herself, so that there could be no chance of any accidental contact—she began to relax.

Slowly they settled into a polite way of dealing with each other, and the immense tension which had filled the room when Cicely had entered it began to return to more manageable levels.

'I want to complete the arrangements for the house-warming ball,' said Mr Evington, when they had dealt with the most pressing letters. 'As you know, I'm holding it towards the end of July. My guests from London will be coming down on the Saturday beforehand. They will spend the week at the Manor, attending the ball on the Friday before leaving again on the following—Saturday—afternoon.'

'Good,' she said briskly, trying her best to behave like a perfect secretary.

'I am going to need some more help around the house when my guests arrive. I've brought enough servants from London with me to cope with the day-to-day running of the Manor, but they won't be able to manage a houseful of guests. Do you know of anyone in the village who might be prepared to come in for a few days and help?'

'I'm sure there are a lot of people,' said Cicely. 'Most of the young men and women from the village would be glad to help out, and then for the ball itself I think you will find most of the local landowners will be happy to lend their own staff. We usually help each other out for big events. Would you like me to deal with it for you?'

'Yes. If you would.'

'I should have it arranged by the end of the week,' she said.

'Now. As to the matter of the croquet . . .'

One by one they dealt with the matters that needed seeing to, and by the end of the day Cicely went back to the Lodge with the feeling of a day well spent. She could not hide from herself the fact that she was enjoying helping out at the Manor, and now that she knew she could do so without a repeat of the disturbing sensations that had struck her when coming close to Mr Evington she could enjoy it in peace.

The Lodge was becoming more home-like with each passing day. Although Cicely still missed living at her beloved Manor she had worked hard to make the Lodge comfortable and welcoming. She had cleaned it thoroughly before she had moved in, and whilst she had not been able to afford to redecorate, she had managed to cover up the worst patches of flaking paint with pictures and mirrors, and to disguise the worn sections of flooring with faded, yet good quality rugs.

She removed her hat as she entered the Lodge, then went through to the sitting-room. She had just thrown open the french windows when Lord Chuffington was announced. Feeling relieved that he had not called half an hour earlier, as she would then have had to invent an excuse as to where she had been, she welcomed him with pleasure.

'What ho! Cicely,' he said, as he ambled into the room in his usual diffident fashion, his hands buried in the pockets of his knife-creased trousers, and his light jacket bunched up behind him.

'Hello, Chuff Chuff.' Cicely greeted him warmly and invited him to sit down.

He took a seat on one of the faded sofas. 'Thought I'd just pop over and see if you were ready for Evington's ball.'

'Not nearly!' exclaimed Cicely, thinking of all the staffing arrangements she had to make. 'There is so much to be done! I have to—' She broke off as she noticed the surprised look on Lord Chuffington's face, and realized that she had almost given away her involvement in the organization of the ball, and therefore her position as Mr Evington's secretary. Chiding herself for being so careless she realized she would have to be more circumspect in future—

in particular she must remember to sound casual when she asked the local landowners to lend their servants, so they did not guess that she was acting as Mr Evington's secretary. 'I have to sort out all my clothes,' she said, changing what she had been about to say into something less revealing.

'Ah! Yes, what!' said Lord Chuffington amiably. He raised and lowered his eyebrows a couple of times and gave her a lackadaisical smile.

Cicely smiled back.

He raised his eyebrows again and Cicely realized that if she wanted the conversation to proceed she would have to provide something to talk about. 'Would you like to see what I've been doing with the garden?' she asked.

'Oh, yes. Rather,' Chuff Chuff beamed.

She led him out through the french doors and into the pretty garden.

'I'm trying to plant it in line with Gertrude Jekyll's ideas,' she said. 'The garden's rather small to let me put them into practice fully, but I want to use her idea of grouping shrubs and flowers so that I have colour in the garden all year round.'

'Jolly good idea,' said Chuff Chuff. He stopped suddenly and turned towards her. With unusual decision—for him!—he said, 'Look here, Cicely old thing, what I mean is, don't you know—that is to say, how about it?'

Cicely was taken aback. 'How about what?'

she asked, scouring her mind in an effort to discover what Chuff Chuff was talking about.

'You know, this marriage lark?' He looked at her with hope in his eyes. 'Can't sit on the shelf for ever, you know. Got to get off it some time. Good Lord, yes! Parmiston's not such a bad old place. And you'd have Antoine.' Antoine was the Chuffingtons' French chef. 'Makes a marvellous kedgeree. And—'

'Chuff Chuff, we've been through this before,' said Cicely with a sigh. 'I—'

'And soufflé,' went on Chuff Chuff, without taking any notice of her. He thrust his hands deeper into his trouser pockets. 'Antoine makes a dashed fine soufflé.' He rocked backwards and forwards on his heels. 'Cheese, and chocolate—not together, you understand—and—'

'Yes,' said Cicely kindly, 'Antoine is a fine chef, and his soufflés are superb, but Chuff Chuff, I can't marry you for a soufflé.'

'Worse reasons to marry a chap,' Chuff Chuff pointed out.

'No, Lord Chuffington, it just won't do,' said Cicely, kind but firm.

'Oh, well. Third time lucky, what?'

Cicely sighed. It was obvious she was not going to be able to persuade Lord Chuffington that she could never marry him. It looked as though she would have to let him propose a third time, after which, perhaps, her refusal might sink in—for much as she liked Chuff

Chuff, and much as marrying him would make her life easier, she had no intention of becoming his wife.

She turned the conversation, therefore, back to the garden, showing him her more notable plants before taking him back inside and offering him some refreshment. He declined, however, saying he was expected back at Parmiston Manor.

Cicely rang the bell and Gibson, looking resplendent in his immaculate butler's uniform, which he insisted on wearing no matter how small the household had become, showed him out.

Cicely gave a rueful smile as she thought over Lord Chuffington's visit. He was a dear, but it was difficult to get through to him sometimes. Ah, well! He would learn in the end, no doubt.

And with that hopeful thought she went upstairs and changed into her cycling outfit. A calf-length divided skirt was so much more practical than a floor-length skirt when she needed to do the weeding!

*   *   *

The next two weeks were busy ones for Cicely. There were a lot of arrangements to be made for Mr Evington's house party, and on top of that she had to find a boy to help Gibson around the house.

The latter proved to be easier than she had expected. Tom, Mrs Johnson's oldest boy, was looking for work, and he soon took up his duties at the Lodge. Cicely's earnings did not allow her to employ him full time, as she also wanted to buy an annuity for Gibson so that he would have some financial security when he retired, but they allowed her to employ him for three mornings a week. Tuesdays, Thursdays and Saturdays were the days she settled upon, they being the mornings which would allow her to keep her employment at the Manor a secret.

Tom quickly became indispensable. He was friendly and willing, and what he lacked in experience he made up for in raw strength and enthusiasm. He fetched and carried, cleaned and polished, he chopped the wood and carried the coal, and all this he did with a cheerful air that made him a pleasure to have around the house.

As the house party at the Manor approached, Cicely spent more of her working hours visiting local families and inveigling them into offering their servants for the occasion, and less of them at the Manor with Mr Evington, for which she was thankful. Although he carefully avoided coming into contact with her, and although Cicely herself made a determined effort never to draw too close to him, being with him had put her under more strain than she cared to admit, even to herself. Her unruly feelings had not subsided as she had hoped they would. If anything, they had grown worse. Every time she was with him her thoughts drifted back to their encounter in the barn, and she seemed to feel his hands on her face and his hot breath on her lips. It therefore came as a relief for her to be able to spend most of her working hours away from him.

Having finally arranged everything to her satisfaction, however, she was forced to spend the last Friday morning before the house party at the Manor, where together she and Mr Evington went through the week's post.

He sat behind his desk as usual and, as he gave her instructions, Cicely could not help noticing the way the sunlight fell across his face, revealing its strength. The line of his jaw and the firmness of his chin gave evidence of his character, and she could understand how he had managed to rise from his humble beginnings to the position he now held. Reluctantly, she found herself coming to respect him. Whilst she might still resent the fact that he had bought her beloved Manor without so much as visiting it first, treating it as a business transaction rather then the purchase of a home, she realized that this same feel for business had enabled him to rise from being a dock hand to being the owner of Oakleigh Manor. She could not help but admire his energy and enterprise. He was so different from the men she usually met, either in Little Oakleigh, or on the one or two occasions when she had visited her aunt in London. They did not move her in any way. They were pleasant and amiable, and utterly unmemorable . . . whilst Mr Evington was unforgettable.

Having dispensed with the last of the letters that had arrived in that morning's post, he leant back in his chair. 'I will be very busy next week, once the house party begins,' he said. 'I won't have time to think about anything except entertaining my guests, so I am giving you a week's holiday.'

Cicely felt a curious mixture of relief and disappointment. The relief she understood, but the disappointment . . . that was something she did not want to understand.

'Very good,' she said, pleased that her voice sounded businesslike, instead of reflecting her contradictory emotions.

'We will carry on as usual once my guests have gone.' He hesitated, as though he was about to say something else, but then a formal mask dropped over his face and the moment was lost. He stood up. 'Until after the ball, then.'

His hand began to rise in a reflex action, as though to shake hers, but then he suddenly dropped it again.

Cicely flushed. From the revealing expression that flashed across his face it was obvious he was remembering the electrical sensation their contact engendered and, damaging as it was to Cicely's peace of mind, she was remembering it, too. She hurriedly gathered up her things, and waiting only to wish him an awkward farewell she swept out of the room. Her exit would have been perfect, if only she had not dropped her notebook. She chided herself inwardly, but it had been inevitable: she had been shaking so much at the memory of what his touch had done to her that she had not been able to keep hold of it.

She bent to pick it up, only to realize that he, too, had bent to retrieve it.

Her face turned towards his as though it was being pulled by an invisible string, and she found her lips almost touching his. Their eyes met, and held. She forgot to breathe, so transfixed was she by the sight of him. His rugged skin was full of light and shadow, and she had to fight an urge to reach out and touch the stubble that was deepening the shadow around his jaw. How would it feel? she wondered. Would it be rough, and prickle against her sensitive fingertips? Or would it be soft and silky, inviting her to touch him even more?

And if she did, how would he react? Would he take her hand and kiss her palm? Would he caress her, as she caressed him? Her mouth dried, and her eyes locked even more deeply on his own.

This was dangerous. She felt the peril, and knew she must resist, regaining control of herself before the situation escalated into something uncontrollable. She tried to speak, knowing she must break the enchantment, but as her lips moved over dry lips, no sound came out.

As his eyes dropped to her mouth she felt a wave of tingles wash all over her body and her eyelids began to close. There was a moment of unbearable anticipation as she waited breathlessly for what was to come . . . and then she felt, rather than saw, him pull away from her. She experienced a moment of frustration, even as her mind felt a wave of relief. And then she heard him say, in a voice so throaty as to be almost unrecognizable, 'Allow me.'

She knew what the effort of speaking had cost him and was determined to play her part in bringing the situation under control. Fighting down the sensations that were threatening to swamp her, she made a decided attempt to salvage the dangerous situation. She would get up; take her things; thank him. And then she would walk out of the room.

She sent the command to her body, but it would not obey. She was held captive by the super-charged force that bound her to him, and when she thought she had risen she found that she had remained as she was.

She saw a battle of emotions playing itself out on his face, and then with a seemingly enormous effort of will he wrested his eyes away from her own and his hands closed around her things.

Cicely, released from the spell that bound her, commanded her body once more to rise. It protested, but at last it obeyed her instructions, and she found herself standing in front of him. But now it was worse. She was so close to him that a piece of paper could not have been slipped between them. They were thigh to thigh, waist to waist, breast to breast. His breath was warm and exciting. As he bent his head towards her it caressed her lips. Her shivers intensified.

And then his hand rose and took her chin. His head angled; her own tilted in response. And then his mouth brushed hers.

The contact sent tingles washing over her from her head to her toes. His touch was so light it was almost non-existent, and it left her wanting more. She swayed towards him, even as a part of her mind, that smallest part that had not yet fully succumbed to his magnetism, saw one of the gardeners, through the window, just coming into view.

But she paid the gardener no heed. She was too bound up in the moment to care about anything else; and whilst her tiniest remaining shred of sanity told her she must step back, and do it quickly, her body refused to listen.

His lips were tantalizing, barely kissing her, and yet they were stirring things inside her she had never experienced before . . .

And then the gardener began to whistle.

Drawing on her last ounce of self-control she stepped back, putting a hand's breadth between them before the gardener could see anything untoward.

Once removed from the heady sensations produced by his mouth pressing so agonizingly lightly against her own, the full horror of the situation began to dawn on her. But whether she was horrified because he had kissed her, or because they had almost been seen by the gardener, she did not know.

Hastily taking the notebook Mr Evington held out to her, she bid him a garbled farewell, and walked out of the room with as much dignity as she could muster.

Once outside, with a closed door between her and her enigmatic employer, her thoughts began to clear. In the barn he had almost kissed her. In the study he had done so.

One thing was now certain, she thought, as she hurried through the hall and out of the front door, if she wanted to retain her sanity she must never, ever let him touch her again.

*   *   *

The arrival of Mr Evington's London guests caused quite a stir in the village. Such a large party of smart people had not been seen in Little Oakleigh for quite some time.

Cicely was relieved that Mr Evington had given her the week off. There would be a lot of cheerful and harmless gossip in the village occasioned by the arrival of Mr Evington's house guests, and knowing how the villagers liked to visit each other on a daily basis when anything exciting happened in Little Oakleigh, Cicely was relieved she would not be away from home. At such a time, her prolonged absences would have been noticed and would have been bound to cause comment.

'Such clothes!' said Mrs Murgatroyd, as she popped in just before lunch. 'No, I won't stay, thank you, I have too much to do, but I had to look in and let you know the news. Three Daimlers have arrived so far, carrying the most elegant people imaginable. Their hats! Feathers and ribbons and goodness knows what! Cicely, you have never seen anything like it. In fact, Little Oakleigh has never seen anything like it. I am beginning to think it is a good thing that Mr Evington moved into the village after all.' Her face suddenly took on a stricken look. 'Oh, Cicely, my dear, I'm so sorry. How thoughtless of me. Of course, I don't mean it's a good thing he moved into the Manor. Any other good size house would have done. But he has brought a breath of fresh air with him. And now that he has recognized he has duties to the village, I think we may make an Oakleighan of him yet.'

She hurried away, ostensibly to visit the

butcher's, but in reality to tell Mrs Sealyham that three Daimlers had arrived.

Her pulses stirred by talk of the visitors, Cicely found it even more difficult than usual to concentrate on her chores, particularly as the smart cars drove past the Lodge on their way up the drive to the Manor. But still, the lunch had to be made, and after that the washing had to be done.

She went into the kitchen, where a smiling Tom was wiping his hands on his trousers.

'Is Gibson back from the shops yet?' she asked him.

'Not yet. But he won't be long,' said Tom. 'I've had a look at the range for you,' he said, standing aside so that Cicely could see the blaze he had lit there. 'Not giving enough hot water, Mr Gibson said, so I've banked it up good and proper.'

'Oh, good,' said Cicely, hearing the fire roar. 'It is such a blessing you know what to do with the range. I am tired of taking lukewarm baths.'

'There'll be plenty of hot water by tonight,' said Tom confidently.

'Thank you, Tom,' said Cicely. She glanced at the clock. It was time for Tom to go.

'Thank you, Miss Haringay. Right, well, I'll be off then.'

And with that he took his leave.

It was not long before Gibson returned from the shops and Cicely looked over the food items as he took them out of the basket. There were sausages and bacon, fruit and vegetables, eggs and cheese, as well as a loaf of bread—everything they needed to see them through the next few days.

'That will do very well, Gibson,' said Cicely.

The door bell rang. Cicely gave an exclamation of annoyance. She really did not want to see anyone else at the moment. She had far too much to do.

'See who it is, Gibson, and if at all possible get them to come back later. I shall never get anything done today at this rate.'

'Very good, miss.'

Gibson slipped on his frock coat and went to answer the door whilst Cicely washed her hands at the sink. A moment later, Gibson returned. 'Mr Evington, miss,' he said.

Cicely froze. Mr Evington? She had expected Mrs Sealyham, or perhaps Mrs Carruthers, come to share the latest news about the guests arriving at the Manor, not the owner of the Manor himself. But if he was here she would have to see him. It could not be avoided. He must have a last-minute problem with the arrangements for the party.

Taking a deep breath, she said, 'Show him into—'

But at that moment, he walked into the kitchen.

'Goodness, Gibson, what do you mean by showing Mr Evington in here?' said Cicely,

124

wondering whether Gibson had taken leave of his senses.

'It's my fault,' said Mr Evington. 'I showed myself in. I didn't want to take up too much of your time.'

'Thank you, Gibson,' said Cicely. 'You may carry on.'

Gibson went out into the garden to pick some herbs for dinner.

Cicely looked at Mr Evington.

'I just wanted—' He broke off as the range began making an ominous banging noise.

Cicely gave an exclamation of vexation, turning to look at it. 'The range is such a nuisance,' she began. 'If it isn't one thing, it's—' But got no further, for Mr Evington had seized hold of her arm.

'Get out of here,' he said. 'Now.'

'But—'

There was time for no more. He opened the back door and pushed her out.

'What?' asked Cicely, as the banging grew louder, but the rest of her sentence was drowned out by the noise.

Mr Evington did not falter. He steered her down the path, and pushed her unceremoniously out of the gate. He had just done so when there came the most almighty explosion from within the house. Cicely turned round in shock. The kitchen window had been blown out and the air was full of the tinkling sound of breaking glass.

'What—?' she asked, turning to him.

'The back boiler,' he said tersely. 'It's exploded.'

'The back boiler exploded?' asked Cicely, still feeling stunned. It had all happened so quickly. The explosion had been terribly loud and the breaking glass had momentarily frightened her; and Mr Evington's man-handling, necessary though it had been, had shaken her nerves.

'The fire was built up way too high,' he said. 'By the look of it the range was an old one. It was inevitable this would happen.'

'But how did you know?' she asked.

'I've seen boilers explode before: I recognized the signs.'

'If you hadn't come in when you did . . .' said Cicely, turning to him, her face white.

'Don't even think about it,' he said.

No, Cicely thought. Better not.

'You're shivering,' he said.

He was right. The shock had taken its toll. She felt suddenly cold.

He took off his coat and wrapped it round her shoulders.

'I'm perfectly all right,' she said. She felt foolish for having given way to shock and did not want him to think her lily-livered—although why it should matter what he thought of her she did not know.

'Of course you are,' he said, leading her over to sit on the grass verge, 'but keep this on anyway.'

Cicely realized it would be useless to protest. And besides, the extra warmth was comforting. It wrapped her round. And so did the scent of Alex Evington. Faint but unmistakable it clung to his jacket, a mixture of expensive cologne and a masculine scent all his own.

At that minute Gibson, looking considerably shaken, emerged from behind the house.

'Ah. Gibson,' said Mr Evington, taking charge of the situation. 'I need you to go and get help. There's going to be a lot of cleaning up to do. Not to mention the risk from the fire.'

'Yes, sir,' said Gibson.

Cicely, about to object to Mr Evington giving Gibson orders, suddenly realized that he had done it in order to settle Gibson's nerves. By giving him something useful to do, Mr Evington had taken his thoughts from the explosion and directed them into more useful channels.

'Right away, sir,' said Gibson, disappearing down the lane.

Are you all right?' asked Mr Evington, taking her hands and chafing them.

'Yes. Just a little shaken, that's all.'

'It's not surprising.'

What was surprising was that, this time, his touch was not electric, it was comforting. She had a sudden longing to rest her head on his shoulder until she had recovered from the shock. She fought against it, and in order to try and divert her thoughts, she asked, 'You say you have seen boilers explode before. Have you had a similar problem with your range?'

'No.' He settled himself more comfortably on the grass beside her, raising one leg in front of him, bent at the knee. 'But I've seen boilers explode on steamships.'

Cicely's interest was caught. She had heard from Alice, courtesy of local neighbourhood gossip, that Mr Evington had worked on steamships. Here was a chance for her to learn more about him. 'You used to work on them?'

'Yes.' He fell silent, and Cicely thought he was not going to say anything else, but then he said, 'I worked on or around ships for much of my early life. I grew up in Liverpool, and when I was a boy it was a good way to make money.'

'Is that why you resent the landed classes so?' she asked. 'Because your early life was hard?' It was a bold question, but she was interested to know.

'No. Not really.'

'Then why?'

He hesitated. 'I . . . have my reasons.'

He was not more forthcoming, and Cicely did not feel equal to questioning him further. But after a few minutes he said, 'Even so, I was wrong to show how I felt. I haven't hidden my dislike very well, I fear.'

'Why should you?' she asked simply.

128

'Good manners?' he suggested humorously.

'There is that,' said Cicely with a smile. Adding wryly, 'But I am not entitled to complain. My own manners have hardly been a model of decorum.'

He took her hands, and she felt a sudden change inside her. His touch was no longer comforting; instead it was stimulating.

Before he could do anything more the villagers, roused by the explosion, started to arrive at the scene. Alice was the first.

'Cicely! Goodness! What happened?' she asked.

'The back boiler,' said Cicely. 'It exploded.'

'No! How awful.' Alice took in the shattered window and the ragged hole that had been torn in the kitchen wall. 'Goodness. What a mess.'

'It is. A terrible mess,' said Mr Evington. He turned back to Cicely. 'You can't stay here,' he said, suddenly practical. 'There is a gaping hole in the wall, and it will take a week to fix it. You will have to come and stay at the Manor.'

'Oh, no,' Cicely protested. 'I couldn't possibly—'

'I won't take no for an answer,' he said firmly. 'There is plenty of room, and the house is prepared for guests. No one would be surprised at you making one of their number, and it would give you somewhere to stay until the Lodge has been repaired.'

'No, I don't think it would be proper—'

Cicely began again, suddenly anxious at the thought of staying beneath the same roof as Mr Evington.

'Miss Babbage, of course, would be invited,' he said. He turned to Alice. 'If you and your mother would do me the honour of accepting an invitation you could keep Miss Haringay company and provide her with a chaperon, as well as, I hope, having an enjoyable time.'

'Oh, yes!' said Alice, her eyes shining, and saying as plainly as words could do, *A week at the Manor, with Mr Evington? Wonderful!*

Cicely looked from one to the other of them, and then back at the ruined side of the Lodge.

She considered her options. On the one hand, she knew that Alice would invite her to stay if she refused Mr Evington's offer; on the other it would put a strain on the Babbages' small household—which consisted of Alice, her mother, a maid of all work and a manservant—to cater for an unexpected guest. Whereas Mr Evington, as he himself had said, was already prepared for guests. And with such a large gathering there could be nothing improper about her accepting his invitation, especially as Alice and her mother were to go as well.

The question was, could she spend a week with Mr Evington and not give way to her unruly feelings, which tempted her to travel down unexplored pathways into a whole new world whenever he was near?

Seeing her hesitate, he organized some privacy for them by saying to Alice, 'If you could retrieve Miss Haringay's shoe?'

Cicely looked down at her right foot. In all the confusion she had barely noticed that she had lost it when being manhandled out of the gate.

'Of course,' said Alice, glad to be of use.

She ran off.

'You need not be afraid of me,' said Mr Evington, looking down into Cicely's eyes and seeking to reassure her. 'If you come to the Manor you will have nothing to fear.'

'I am not afraid of you,' she said. But her voice caught in her throat.

'No?'

There was a sudden tension in the air.

She swallowed. 'No.' She almost said, I am afraid of myself, but managed to stop herself just in time. But it was true, she was afraid of herself. When she was with Mr Evington she discovered parts of herself that she had not known existed. He had touched something inside her that had been lying dormant, and though it was wonderful to experience the new and scintillating feelings he awakened inside her, it was alarming as well.

'Then you have no reason to refuse my invitation to stay at the Manor,' he said.

'You are very kind.'

His mouth quirked humorously, as though

131

kindness was not the motivation for his offer.

Is it wise? she asked herself, before committing herself to an answer. But wise or not she had no real alternative. 'Thank you. I accept.'

'There is one thing.' He hesitated.

'Yes?'

'If you are to be my guest, you can't go on calling me Mr Evington.'

She felt a shiver of apprehension. She knew what he was going to say next.

'You must call me Alex.'

There was something intimate about the notion, and she knew that it would make it harder for him to treat him with the distant manner necessary. And yet it was unavoidable.

'And at the party you must call me Cicely,' she said.

'Cicely.' His voice was soft and sultry.

Fortunately for Cicely's composure, at that moment Alice returned, bearing her shoe.

'I've checked to make sure there's no glass in it,' she said.

'Thank you.' Cicely tried—with little success—to dismiss the memory of Alex's voice as it had caressed her name, and slipped the shoe back on her foot.

'Miss Haringay has accepted my invitation,' said Mr Evington, standing up. 'I hope you and your mother will do the same.'

'I'm sure we will,' said Alice, her voice filled with excitement.

132

'Then I will expect you as soon as I see you. I will return to the Manor and tell the housekeeper to make up rooms for three more guests. Oh, and of course you must bring Gibson,' he said to Cicely. 'He, too, will need somewhere to stay. In fact, I am sure he would be very useful in the coming week, as well as very welcome—that is, if you have no objection to his helping out?'

'No. None.'

He looked down the lane, to where a group of people were converging on the Lodge. 'The local officials can take over now,' he said.

Cicely slipped his jacket from her shoulders as he stood up. She handed it back to him, knowing she must not detain him. He took it, swinging it over his shoulder. As he did so, Cicely's eyes were drawn to the sight of his muscles working beneath his shirt, and she was filled with a sudden desire to feel his arms around her once again. But such a thought was madness. No good would come of such ideas, and she must banish them from her mind.

'Miss Haringay,' he said politely. 'Miss Babbage.' Then making the ladies a slight bow he walked away.

Cicely's eyes followed him down the drive—until she realized what they were doing, whereupon she forced her attention back to the pressing matter in hand. And it was pressing. She gave a deep sigh. She must now deal with the aftermath of the explosion.

An hour later, explanations had been made and workers organized to assess the damage with a view to carrying out the repairs. She had made no mention of the fact that Tom had stoked the fire too high when asked about the cause of the explosion, she had simply blamed it on the back boiler being old. Tom had been doing his best to help, and a quiet word in private would make sure he knew the risks involved in making the fire too hot so that he would not do it again. That way, he would not be embarrassed or have to feel guilty about the incident, which he had never intended.

Then came the task of cleaning up the mess the explosion had left in its wake. It seemed to take forever to sort things out, despite the number of willing helpers who lent a hand, but at last it was done. The repairs to the Lodge, however, would take longer. Cicely sighed. She had been hoping perhaps at a later date to employ a maid to help her in the house for one day a week, but now anything left over from her wages would have to go on setting the Lodge to rights.

Still, there was no use in repining. She was fortunate that she did not have to worry about having a roof over her head for the coming week: Mr Evington had seen to that. In one way at least, she no longer dreaded it—she had now visited the Manor so many times since moving out of it that she could go back as a guest without being troubled by the situation, and knowing that Gibson was also welcome took a great weight off her mind—but in another way it filled her with apprehension. Mr Evington had said she had nothing to fear from him. But living in the same house as him, sleeping under the same roof—who knew what complications it would bring?

*   *   *

What shall I wear? thought Cicely an hour later, as she looked at her few good clothes, which she had spread out on the bed. True, they were well made and, having been bought before she had known her father had run up such huge debts, they had been expensive. But still, they were too few to last her for seven days.

But clothes were the least of her problems, she reminded herself. The range had been destroyed, and half of the kitchen with it. She would just have to make her outfits do.

Leaving Tom to wheel her valise round to the Manor on the hand cart, she set out to walk up the drive. As she approached the Manor she saw what a difference had already come over it. Three smart motor cars were parked in the turning circle, which in her father's time had seen nothing faster than a carriage. The sound of chatter and laughter floated out of the open windows. Steeling herself to face a throng of unknown people,

135

Cicely rang the bell.

The door was opened by the butler, and to Cicely's relief she saw that the hall was all but empty. She would have some time to adjust to being at the Manor before meeting the rest of Mr Evington's guests, it seemed.

She was greeted politely, and shown up to one of the guest rooms.

It seemed strange not to be sleeping in her old room, but in a way she was glad. It would have raised too many echoes of the past. The guest room was small, but overlooked the front of the house. Cicely was just opening the window when Alice bounded in.

'I say, Cicely, isn't this wonderful!' she exclaimed, as she looked round the room. 'Quite like old times.'

'Old times were never like this,' teased Cicely 'A houseful of guests, and an army of servants to wait on them.'

'Well, no, your father never did like entertaining.' She paused. 'Is it very difficult for you, being at the Manor again?' she asked cautiously.

'No. I have grown used to it,' said Cicely. She gave Alice an affectionate smile, and her eyes twinkled. 'So you are free to enjoy yourself!'

'Oh, Cicely, I'm so pleased. I wouldn't have wanted to be happy if you were not, but it is rather wonderful. All the people and all the glamour. Mother is so excited.'

'Where is she?' enquired Cicely.

'In the east wing. In fact, Mother has had an idea.'

Cicely looked at Alice enquiringly.

About our evening dresses. I only have three, and I know you're the same, but it is mother's idea that if we swap them between ourselves we will each end up with six different gowns to wear.'

'And as we are only here for seven evenings, that means a different gown for nearly every evening,' said Cicely, delighted with the idea.

And not only that. Mother has raided her workbasket and found several lengths of lace, together with a selection of silk flowers and a number of ribbon bows. By adding a few extra trims to each gown, or indeed by removing a few, she can make them seem different.'

'What a splendid notion,' said Cicely 'Unless anyone is looking closely, they are not likely to notice that the green silk gown I wear on Monday is the same as the green silk you wear on Friday, particularly if it has a different trim. We will appear to be as well dressed as any of the other guests.'

Apart from our lack of morning dresses and tea gowns,' giggled Alice.

Cicely smiled. 'We will just have to hope Mr Evington's guests are more interested in their own appearances than ours.' At that moment the gong was struck in the hall. 'Goodness! I'd forgotten how loud it sounds,' said Cicely, who had left the gong behind when she had moved to the Lodge.

'Time to dress for dinner,' said Alice. 'I will see you downstairs.'

She ran lightly out of the room, almost bumping into a neat little maid who had just arrived.

'The master's compliments, miss,' said the maid to Cicely as Alice departed. 'I've come to help you dress.'

Cicely felt a warm feeling wash over her at this evidence of Mr Evington's—Alex's—unexpected thoughtfulness. He really was a most surprising man.

'Thank you,' she said.

With the help of the maid she washed and changed, putting on one of her three evening gowns. It was an exquisite creation, made for Cicely by a talented local dressmaker who had once worked for the great Doucet in Paris. Made of the palest pink chiffon it floated around her delicate curves as she dropped it over her head. The maid arranged it over her lace-trimmed petticoat before fastening it at the back, whereupon it draped itself elegantly around Cicely's trim waist before flowing down over her hips and falling in a swirling cascade to the floor.

The maid then arranged her hair in a simple pompadour, piling her hair on top of her head and leaving her neck and shoulders bare.

There came a knock at the door, and Alice

entered. She was dressed in a gown of pale primrose brocade, her slender waist accentuated with a white sash.

'Are you ready to go down?' she asked.

Cicely fastened a pair of pearl ear-rings in her ears and pulled on her long white evening gloves. 'I am.'

Cicely was apprehensive as they went downstairs. Although she had accustomed herself to being at the Manor when she worked there, it was different to visit it *en fête*. The hall below her was full of the most elegant people. The ladies in exquisite evening gowns, all décolletée and swishing trains, conversed with smartly attired gentlemen in evening dress. The gay conversation met Cicely and Alice at the half landing. Bright bursts of laughter punctuated the hubbub, and there was an atmosphere of enjoyment and good humour.

'This is how the Manor was meant to be,' murmured Cicely. For a moment she was transported back in time, to the days of her early childhood when her mother had been alive. Her parents had often entertained then, and thrown parties that were the talk of the neighbourhood. But after her mother's death her father had retreated into his own hobbies, and had cut off all but the most basic contact with the outside world.

Cicely and Alice reached the bottom of the stairs and were joined by Mrs Babbage, who

139

was evidently enjoying herself. She had dressed herself in her best clothes and was making the most of the unexpected frivolity.

'Isn't it wonderful?' breathed Alice, looking round at all the lace and jewels in awe.

They went through into the drawing-room, where Cicely's eye was drawn irresistibly to Alex. Immaculately dressed in a black tailcoat, wing-collared shirt, bow tie and tailored trousers, he looked magnificent. His dark hair was brushed back from his face, revealing the masculine lines of his cheek and jaw. He had more character than anyone Cicely had ever met, and it showed on his face, being etched into the lines around his eyes to give his face interest and depth.

And then her eyes drifted to his companion and her heart stopped, for next to Alex was a statuesque beauty who held herself like a queen, and who was holding on to his arm with a distinctly proprietorial air.

Cicely felt a twist inside her. She was totally unprepared for it, and only just managed to stifle a gasp. What was the cause of that sudden twist? Surely it could not be jealousy? No, of course not. What reason had she to be jealous? Alex was entitled to offer his arm to one of his guests—indeed, good manners made it imperative that he do so. He was even entitled to be in love with the full-figured beauty, she told herself, noting the way his arm encircled the Amazon's waist. And besides,

Cicely told herself, she could not possibly be jealous, because Alex was nothing to her. Nothing but an acquaintance, a man who had, by coincidence, bought a house she had offered for sale, and then employed her as his secretary. Yes, that was all, she told herself determinedly.

At that moment he turned and saw her. A warm smile washed over his face, and it lit Cicely inside. Against all reason she was delighted that he was pleased to see her.

Excusing himself to his companion, he walked across the drawing-room to welcome her.

'Cicely, I'm so pleased you could come.' His eyes lingered on her face. Then, as if remembering himself, he turned to Alice and her mother and made them welcome.

'Oh, we are so pleased to be here!' said Alice, looking up at him adoringly.

Mrs Babbage was similarly smitten, though she was better at hiding it than her daughter.

'Let me introduce you to some of my other guests.'

He introduced them to the statuesque beauty, Miss Postlethwaite. With her elegantly coiffured dark hair, voluptuous figure, great height and majestic bearing, she reminded Cicely of the Wertheimer sisters, whose likeness had been caught so well by the painter John Singer Sargent a few years earlier. Like them, Miss Postlethwaite was the epitome of elegance and glamour. Miss Postlethwaite greeted them politely, before moving gracefully away to talk to the other guests.

More introductions followed, and Cicely soon found herself the centre of a group of agreeable people, all of whom knew nothing of her exploding range and accepted her as just another of Alex's guests.

'If you'll allow me,' said Mr Stirling to Cicely, as the dinner gong rang. 'I'm to have the pleasure of taking you into dinner.'

'Of course,' said Cicely politely, her eyes unconsciously straying to Alex, who was escorting an elderly dowager into the dining-room. She felt her spirits lift. How stupid of her, to be so affected by such a little thing. For she had thought he would go into dinner with Miss Postlethwaite, and was ridiculously pleased when he did not.

Alice and Mrs Babbage were similarly escorted into the dining-room, and all three ladies took their places at the long table.

Mr Stirling was good company, and he and Cicely passed the meal pleasantly by talking about their favourite books.

'I didn't know you were a fan of Sherlock Holmes,' said Alex, joining Cicely after dinner, when coffee was served in the drawing-room.

His eyes looked teasingly into her own.

'Oh. Yes, I am,' said Cicely. She and Mr Stirling had talked about the splendid stories over dinner, and Mr Stirling had obviously mentioned the fact to Alex.

'I didn't notice any of Conan Doyle's stories in the library,' he said.

Cicely gave a mischievous smile. 'That's because I took them all with me!'

He laughed. 'How are you settling in at the Manor? he asked. 'Is your room to your liking? I haven't had a chance to ask you before now.'

'Yes, thank you, it is.'

'Because if you would like another one you have only to say.'

'No. I am very comfortable where I am.'

He was about to speak when one of his guests hailed him from across the room. 'I say, Evington, what about a game of billiards?'

'I'm afraid that will be impossible,' he said.

'Impossible? Pish!' said the young man. 'Nothing's impossible.'

'I'm afraid this is. You see, there's no billiard room.'

'What? No billiard room. Good Lord! You'll have to hurry up and build one then.'

Cicely turned away. In one way she could not take exception to what the young man had said: most country houses had billiard rooms. But it hurt her to have the Manor's inadequacies spoken of. She knew it needed bringing up to date, but she loved it anyway, and although she could now enter it without feeling a loss of spirits, and had indeed enjoyed seeing it *en fête,* she did not like to hear it belittled.

Looking up, she caught Alex's eye in the mirror. He was looking at her curiously, as though wondering what had brought the sudden look of pain to her face. But there was more than curiosity in his eyes. There was an unmistakable gleam of tender concern as well.

Fortunately, Alice came up to her at that moment and distracted her, forcing her to break eye contact with Alex and give her attention to the other guests. Otherwise she might have been guilty of giving way to wholly inappropriate feelings . . . feelings that were becoming increasingly hard to deny.

She saw no more of Alex that evening and, as she undressed for bed later that evening she was grateful for it, because as she finally blew out the candle—the gas lighting not reaching this part of the house—she realized that staying at the Manor was going to cause her difficulties she had not foreseen. Not only was it going to bring her into contact with Alex every single day, but it was also going to force her to acknowledge her unfortunate reaction to the beautiful Miss Postlethwaite, whose statuesque image haunted her until she fell asleep.

CHAPTER SEVEN

Alex was up early the following morning. Although most of his guests thought the forthcoming ball was nothing more than a house-warming gesture, there was one person who knew that it had been arranged in order to snare the man who had almost ruined his sister's life by framing her for a theft she didn't commit. That person was Miss Eugenie Postlethwaite—or, as she was more usually and correctly known, Mrs Eugenie Dortmeyer.

Alex went down to the library as soon as he was dressed. He had arranged to meet Eugenie at half past seven, and as the long-case clock struck the half-hour the door opened and Eugenie, looking magnificent in a long tailored skirt and high-necked blouse, entered the room.

'Eugenie.' Alex smiled. Taking her hands, he kissed her on the cheek. 'It was good of you to get out of bed so early. I thought we had better meet at this hour so that we would not be in any danger of being interrupted by any of the other guests.'

Eugenie returned his greeting. 'I understand.'

'In fact, it was good of you to come to the house party at all,' he said, indicating a chair for Eugenie and then, when she had settled, sitting down himself. 'Especially at such short notice.'

'To help you catch that rat I'd have come a lot further,' she said, not mincing her words. 'And done it at the drop of a hat.'

There was a hint of an American twang in her voice. After growing up in the same neighbourhood as Alex, Eugenie had set out to explore the world. She had fallen in love with, and eventually married, Hyram Dortmeyer, an American magnate, and now spent most of her time in Boston or London. But she had responded to Alex's plea for help and had been only too happy to join him at the Manor.

She ran her eyes appreciatively round Alex's study, taking in the splendid bookshelves and large mahogany desk before turning to look out of the french windows. 'You've found a beautiful place here,' she said, as her eyes roved over the sweeping lawns.

'Yes. It's perfect.'

'It's lucky your Miss Haringay had to sell.'

'*My* Miss Haringay?' He raised his eyebrows. 'She is not *my* Miss Haringay.'

'No?' Eugenie gave him a knowing look.

He spoke firmly. 'No.'

'That's funny. From the way you were looking at her—' began Eugenie.

'And what do you mean by that?' he interrupted.

She laughed. Why, nothing, Alex . . . except

that every time you looked at her your eyes smouldered and your hands clenched, as though you wanted to sweep her off her feet and carry her up to the bedroom,' remarked Eugenie with a mischievous twinkle in her eye.

Alex gave an exasperated sigh. 'Ever since you've married you've become incorrigible,' he said.

'I have, haven't I?' she asked innocently. 'Marriage does that to a person.' She twinkled at him. 'You should try it yourself.'

He laughed. 'If I thought I'd be as happy as you and Hyram I'd marry tomorrow.'

Eugenie was unperturbed. 'You would be.'

'Oh, no, Genie, you've got it all wrong,' he said, shaking his head. 'Even if I asked Miss Haringay to marry me tomorrow—which I have no intention of doing—she would not have me. Miss Haringay regards me as a cross between a Philistine and Attila the Hun!'

'Really? I haven't seen that in her face when she looks at you. What I've seen is her looking at you as though you're forbidden fruit: tempting, but dangerous,' she said.

He shook his head. 'You couldn't be more mistaken.'

'What makes you so sure she doesn't like you?' asked Eugenie curiously.

'First of all, because I knocked her off her bicycle and then laughed at her when she fell into the duck pond—'

'In that case, I'm not surprised!' laughed

Eugenie.

'Secondly, because I wouldn't let the Sunday school hold their picnic here—'

'That's not like you,' said Eugenie, surprised. 'You're usually so thoughtful where other people are concerned. Especially children.'

'Not when I have a lot on my mind,' Alex admitted. 'And not when I'm ordered to do it by a busybody who hardly lets me unpack before ordering me about. And thirdly—'

'Yes?'

'Thirdly . . .' A shadow crossed his face. 'She doesn't like cits.'

Eugenie raised her fine eyebrows. 'You don't say? She seemed to be getting on along just fine with Mr Benson last night, and you can't get more of a cit than Benson.'

'Did she?' asked Alex, his brows drawing together.

'But that would mean nothing to you, of course,' remarked Eugenie lightly; nevertheless interested to see how black his brow had become at the idea of Cicely being charming to another gentleman.

'No.' Alex spoke through gritted teeth. 'Of course not.'

Eugenie shook her head. 'Face it, Alex! If you're not in love with her already, you soon will be.' Then, seeing he had had enough teasing for one day, she said, 'But that's enough for now. I've had my fun. I didn't come here to tease you about Miss Haringay—although I have to admit, I've kind of enjoyed it! Still, I came here to help you catch a thief.'

Alex gave a sigh of relief. Some of Eugenie's remarks about Miss Haringay had been too close for comfort. 'Yes. A thief. The Honourable—'

Eugenie snorted. 'More like *dis*honourable.'

'. . . Martin Goss.'

Eugenie looked appreciatively round the room again. 'The Manor's the perfect place to catch him.'

Alex stood up and strode over to the fireplace. 'It is. It's the perfect setting in which to spring the trap, and it's near enough to Goss's own place to make it seem natural for me to invite him—he can just, without too big a stretch of the imagination, be considered to be one of my new neighbours.'

'And he's accepted the invitation, you say?' asked Eugenie.

'Yes.' Alex gave a twisted smile. 'The Honourable Martin will be delighted to attend.'

'Then we've got him.' Eugenie spoke with confidence.

'Not yet,' said Alex cautiously. 'There's still a long way to go before we can say that. But we're well on the way.'

'And what about the necklace?'

'I'm picking it up from the jewellers tomorrow. I meant to go yesterday, but . . .'—

he hesitated, as he thought of Cicely's exploding range—'something came up. Still, you'll have it in time for dinner that evening. It will then have a chance to excite gossip, and once Goss hears about it he'll be sure to want to steal it. He's in low funds at the moment, and he needs something to get him out of the clutches of the moneylenders. The necklace will appear like a Godsend to him.'

Eugenie sighed. 'It's just a pity Hyram couldn't be here,' she said. 'He would have loved to see us catch the rat. But it wasn't a good idea.'

Alex agreed. 'Not after his being at a house party where a diamond tie pin went missing a year ago. If Goss were to see him here he might recognize him and decide another theft would be too big a risk.'

'Which is why I'm using my maiden name,' agreed Eugenie. 'Otherwise Goss might recognize the name, and worry about me telling Hyram all about it. He might decide that Hyram could put two and two together and realize he's the thief who's been plaguing society for the last five years, and decide not to steal anything, just to be safe. And after all our careful planning, that would not suit us at all.'

'No. It wouldn't. I want to catch him, Eugenie, and hand him over to the authorities so that he'll be made to pay for what he did to Katie—and, incidentally, to make sure he doesn't do it to any other innocent young girl.

For the duration of the party you will be Miss Postlethwaite—' his eyes twinkled '—proud possessor of a fabulous necklace.' He stood up. 'I should be back from the jewellers by three o'clock, but to be on the safe side I suggest you meet me here at four. I will hand over the necklace, and you, my dear Eugenie, will wear it every day until it's stolen.'

*   *   *

Cicely, having finished her breakfast, was putting the finishing touches to her toilette. Being Sunday, the assembled company was going to church, and Cicely was to be one of their number. The one relief for her was that, having her own pew, she would not have to sit anywhere near Mr Evington, because her feelings for him were becoming so confused that she did not want to spend any more time in his company than was strictly necessary.

As she settled her plumed hat on her head she realized that her feelings towards him had been softening for some time; in fact, ever since she had taken a job as his secretary. The interest he had shown in her father's collection had warmed her, and made it clear that he was not just a hard-headed and hard-hearted businessman, but that he was a man of sensitivity as well. She had been afraid that he would deride her father's collection and order the boneshakers to be thrown away, but instead he had shown a real enjoyment of the various contraptions her father had collected, and had made it clear he intended to produce a catalogue for them—something her father had always wanted to do.

Then, too, there had been other feelings that had arisen during her time as his secretary, notably those that had coursed through her when he had fallen on top of her in the barn . . . She turned her thoughts away from such distracting channels, forcing herself to forget the lightning bolt that had shot through her as his weight had pressed down on her, and his face had hovered mere inches from his own.

But her recalcitrant mind, having been forced out of that channel, went down another one equally distracting, recalling the feelings that had flooded her being when the range had exploded. Not only had his gentleness made her go weak at the knees, but his behaviour had shown her what it was like to have someone she could rely on, something she had never had in the course of her short life. Indeed, quite the opposite. She had been the one who had had to be reliable. Her father, dear though he had been, had in many ways been more like a child than a grown man, and he had always looked to her to see to the practicalities of life; and since his death the burden of sorting out the muddle he had left behind had fallen entirely on her. So it had come as a surprise to her to find that she had someone to rely on, someone whose shoulders had carried the burden for her when events had unexpectedly taken a turn for the worse. She gave a slight shiver. For it was not only the strength of his personality she remembered, but the strength of his body: the sight of his muscles rippling beneath his shirt when he had thrown his jacket over his shoulder, and the feel of his arms as he had wrapped them comfortingly around her.

But this would not do. She was meant to be turning her thoughts away from memories of Alex, and not dwelling on them. All in all, she felt it would be better if she saw as little of possible of him over the coming week.

Fortunately, for that day at least, it was easier than she had expected. Flanked by Alice and Mrs Babbage she managed to walk to the church without saying more than a few polite words to him, and during the service she occupied her usual pew, which meant that she was well away from Alex and his other guests. And afterwards, again flanked by Alice and Mrs Babbage, she managed to return to the Manor without talking to him once.

At luncheon she was similarly fortunate. He was seated at the other end of the table, and once luncheon was finished she managed to select activities at which he was not present. By careful management she managed to avoid him that evening, and on the morrow she managed to do the same . . . at least to begin with: the morning was spent in her room, and after lunch Alex excused himself to his guests by saying he had some urgent business to attend to in town.

At this news, Cicely gave a sigh of relief. The visit was turning out to be less difficult than she had expected. If all went well she should be able to emerge unscathed when the house party ended in just under a week.

In the meantime, she, too, had business to attend to. She wanted to walk down to the Lodge and see how the repairs were coming along.

Reassuring Alice and Mrs Babbage that she did not need their company she set off down the drive. The builders—local village men, trustworthy and reliable—were hard at work, and told her they expected to finish the job by the end of the week. Cicely was relieved. At least now she would have a house to return to when the party came to an end. It was with a spring in her step, therefore, that she returned to the Manor.

The summery sound of leather on willow greeted her as she walked up the drive, and she realized there must be a cricket match going on. As she rounded a bend this was confirmed by the sight of the gentlemen, in their white flannels, playing the traditional game. They made an attractive spectacle against the green of the lawns, which Cicely had to admit were far better tended under Alex's care then they ever had been under her father's: Alex had had them neatly cut and edged in preparation for the party.

Underneath the chestnut tree, a number of ladies were watching the game. Cicely looked for Alice and Mrs Babbage, but her friends did not appear to be spectating. They would be in Alice's room, she guessed, altering their evening dresses.

She crossed the terrace and headed towards the side door, intending to join them so that she could alter her pale pink chiffon gown, making it a little different so that Alice could wear it in a few days' time. But as she passed the study something flew past her ear and fell with a thud into the flower bed. She looked round, startled, but on seeing old Mr Hart running towards her she realized it must have been the cricket ball. She was about to walk on, so as not to interfere with the game, when she noticed that Mr Hart was clutching his side. He was puffing and blowing, and she decided he needed a bit of help. Abandoning the idea of not interfering, she lifted her skirt an inch or two and stepped daintily across the flower bed in the direction of the thud.

'Oh, Alex, it's the most beautiful thing I've ever seen!'

The words drifted out of the open french windows.

Cicely looked up, surprised. Just inside the

155

windows, their backs towards her, were Eugenie Postlethwaite and Alex.

Cicely felt her heart beginning to beat faster. Eugenie was holding aside a few stray tendrils that had escaped from her fashionable pompadour hairstyle and Alex was fastening the most exquisite emerald necklace round her neck.

Cicely watched, transfixed, as Eugenie turned to face him, arranging the necklace across her high-necked blouse.

'It's enchanting!' said Eugenie with stars in her eyes. She kissed Alex on the cheek.

Cicely coloured to the roots of her hair. She had unwittingly stumbled on to an intimate scene, and now that the first shock was over she wanted to get away as quickly as possible. Her limbs started to come back under her control. Thank goodness neither Mr Evington nor Miss Postlethwaite had seen her, she thought, as she turned away from the window. She looked round for the ball, seizing it as soon as she laid eyes on it, then hastily she returned to the terrace.

Mr Hart was approaching her, and Cicely was relieved to see that his hand was no longer clutching his side.

'Thank you, my dear,' he said with a gasp. 'I'm not as young as I was, I fear.'

Cicely handed him the ball with a fixed smile and an encouraging word, which sounded unnaturally strained to her own ears.

Mr Hart, however, appeared to notice nothing untoward, and was entirely taken in by her apparently natural manner. Taking the ball he returned to the game, leaving Cicely to hurry into the Manor.

It is none of my business, she told herself, as her mind replayed the events she had witnessed in the study. It was only by the most unlucky chance that she had seen and heard anything untoward, and she must forget about it at once.

But she could not forget. She could not wipe away the memory of Eugenie's look of joy when Alex had given her the necklace, or the kiss Eugenie had bestowed on his cheek.

Her own cheeks burned as she thought of it, but she must not dwell on it. She must drive the image away.

With a determined effort she managed to do so, but her thoughts then went to the reasons behind the scene she had witnessed, and she felt her stomach twist. There could be only one reason why Alex had been giving Eugenie such a valuable piece of jewellery: they must be about to announce their engagement. Either that, or . . . Cicely flushed, as she remembered that fashionable house parties often provided illicit lovers with a chance to meet and indulge their passion. Could that be the explanation for what she had seen?

Cicely took a firm grip on herself. Whatever

157

the reason, it was none of her business. She must not allow herself to think about it. Alex's private life was his own affair. It was not her concern. Telling herself that the twist she felt in her stomach was nothing more than indigestion she continued into the Manor. She fought down an urge to go to her own room, where she had the inexplicable feeling that her spirits would sink still further, and went instead to Alice's room: some cheerful company and useful occupation were just what she needed. There, sure enough, Alice and Mrs Babbage were hard at work altering the dresses they had worn the evening before.

'Cicely,' said Alice, looking up. 'You're just in time! We were wondering what you would think of adding a lace frill to your pink chiffon.'

Cicely looked at the dress critically as Alice held a band of lace around its neckline.

'Yes,' she said. 'I think that would be a good idea. It doesn't seem out of place, and makes the dress look quite different.'

Pulling out her hatpin and putting it on the dressing-table, Cicely laid her hat beside it and then set to work.

The three ladies spent the next hour cutting and sewing, adding frills, removing flounces and attaching silk flowers, until the dresses they had already worn had been altered in some slight but noticeable way.

'There,' said Cicely, looking at her pale-pink

158

gown when she had finished. It now had a wide flounce of lace around its neck-line, and a similar trimming round its hem.

'It looks quite different,' said Alice, pleased. She held up her own delicate primrose gown, which had been adorned with silk flowers.

'Very good,' said Mrs Babbage looking closely. 'It will not fool someone who has been looking at your clothes closely, of course, but to the casual observer your gowns will appear to be new, particularly as you will be swapping them between you, and wearing them three or four days apart.'

Mrs Babbage, too, had altered her gown. She had removed the train, which had been attached at the shoulder, and had removed the sleeves. It would not pass close inspection, but with luck it would be taken for a new outfit; something she was feminine enough to be pleased about.

'And now I suggest we go out and watch the cricket,' she said.

Cicely and Alice agreed. By this time Cicely had regained control of her emotions, and she was determined not to let her foolishness spoil the joys of the party for Alice and Mrs Babbage. She would have to spend the next five days in Mr Evington's company, it was true, but given his interest in Miss Postlethwaite it was unlikely she would see very much of him.

Leaving her to wonder why, when the

prospect was so satisfactory, it gave her no pleasure, but instead gave her only pain.

* * *

The succeeding days quickly fell into a regular pattern. In the mornings the ladies kept to their rooms, writing letters or gossiping, or—in the case of Cicely's party—altering their evening gowns. In the afternoons the guests, both ladies and gentlemen, played croquet or tennis, or sat beneath the spreading chestnut trees that dotted the lawn, enjoying the shade. And in the evenings they met for dinner, and afterwards whiled away the time by playing bridge.

Cicely saw little of Alex. He was a courteous host and enquired after her welfare several times, but his manner was distant and he spent most of his time with Miss Postlethwaite, so that Cicely was relieved when her week at the Manor came to an end. She had only to endure the ball, she told herself on the Friday morning, and then it would all be over. On the following morning she could go back to the Lodge, which had now been repaired, and forget all about Alex—at least, until Monday morning, when she would have to take up her duties again.

'I'm so glad we saved our best gowns for this evening,' said Alice as she wafted into Cicely's room, dressed in a beautiful dress of lavender tulle with a delectably swishing train. 'I would not have liked to wear an altered gown tonight.'

Both girls had saved their best dresses for the festivity. Cicely was already dressed in a most beautiful gown. Cut off the shoulder with narrow ribbon straps to hold it in place, it was the height of elegance. It was made of pale-blue *mousseline de soie* which perfectly suited Cicely's ash-blonde hair and fair complexion, bringing out echoing flashes of blue in her grey eyes. The silky fabric draped itself elegantly around her feminine curves. It was nipped in at the waist with a decorative sash before flaring out into a long skirt which trailed elegantly into a flounced train.

Cicely pulled on her long gloves and accompanied Alice downstairs, together with Mrs Babbage. As she reached the foot of the staircase, she was glad she was wearing her best gown. It gave her a boost of confidence, for which she was grateful, as the idea of watching Alex drifting round the ballroom with Miss Postlethwaite in his arms filled her with unaccountable dread.

She had no time to dwell on it, however, as the guests from the surrounding neighbourhood were already beginning to arrive. Most of them were old friends, and she was soon absorbed in interesting conversations about local life.

And then the music started. Her hand was

claimed by Roddy, who had clearly been enjoying the house party, and after that it was claimed by Lord Chuffington. Chuff Chuff was looking splendid in evening dress. He was a good dancer, being light on his feet, and Cicely found it a pleasure to be whirled around the floor by him.

More dances followed, and then, just as she left the floor with Mr Carruthers, she found herself whisked back on to it as the orchestra struck up the opening chords of a waltz.

'May I have the pleasure?' asked Alex, smiling down into her eyes as one arm glided round her waist whilst the other took her hand in a firm, sure grasp.

'It seems I have no choice,' said Cicely apprehensively. Although she knew that dancing with Alex would be glorious, she also knew it would not be wise.

'Only object, and I will escort you to the side of the room,' he said teasingly.

For one moment she almost asked him to do so, but the temptation to feel his arm around her was too much for her and she smiled, caution forgotten as she looked up into his velvety brown eyes. 'I fear, I cannot.'

He laughed, then, settling his arm more possessively round her waist, he whirled her on to the floor. Cicely had just enough time to catch up her train before they joined the other dancers. His hold was so sure, his guiding arm so strong, that she felt herself relax.

'And how are you enjoying the ball?' he asked. 'You are not sorry I persuaded you to come?'

'Persuaded?' she laughed. As I remember it, you traded with me!'

'So I did. Well? Was it a bad deal?'

'I will let you know after the Sunday school picnic,' she teased him.

He laughed. 'Which has been organized for the last week in September, as usual,' he said. 'But you still haven't answered my question. Are you enjoying the ball?'

She hesitated. To admit that she was seemed dangerous, and yet in all honesty how could she do anything else? 'Yes, I am,' she said.

'Good.'

There was a profound satisfaction in his voice, far more so than she would have expected, and it sent a tingle down her spine. It made her suddenly aware of the fact that, in keeping with current fashions, her shoulders and much of her back was bare, and she hoped he had not felt the tingle as it passed through her.

Whether he had or not she could not tell, but the pressure of his hand in the small of her back increased and she felt a smouldering heat radiating outwards from his touch. It spread, imbuing her shoulders and neck with a delicate flush. She had a sudden urge to pull away from him and run out of the ballroom, coupled with an equally strong yet contradictory wish that he would pull her closer still. It was these kind of confusing thoughts that made it so difficult for her to be with Alex, and yet made it so wonderful at the same time.

'And how have the repairs been coming along at the Lodge?'

'Very well,' she said, glad to seize on this ordinary topic of conversation. Having Alex's arms around her was proving even more unsettling than she had anticipated, and the practicalities of the Lodge formed a much-needed diversion. 'The kitchen has been thoroughly cleaned and the hole in the wall has been repaired. The range itself has been disposed of, as unfortunately it was beyond rescue.'

'A good thing. It was old and unsafe.'

Cicely sighed. A good thing in a way, perhaps, but in another way a sad blow, because now she would have to find the money to replace it.

He looked at her in concern. 'What's wrong?' he asked.

'Oh, nothing,' she said quickly. She had no desire for him to learn how impecunious she was.

He looked at her closely. 'If something is worrying you, I hope you know you can tell me,' he said. 'If you need any help—'

'No, of course not, what help could I possibly need? It is simply that . . .'

'Yes?' he asked.

She thought hard for an excuse. She did not like misleading him, and yet her pride demanded that she come up with some innocuous reason for her sigh.

'It's just that it seems such a pity the party will be over tomorrow.' Adding hastily, in case she had sounded forward, and not wanting him to read anything particular into it, 'Alice was saying so as we came downstairs, and her mother and I both agree.'

He looked at her intently, as though realizing she was hiding something, but then decided not to press her. 'I'm glad you feel that way. And Alice and her mother, too,' he added with a wicked smile.

The music drew to a close. Alex bowed over her hand then led her to the side of the room. Cicely's heart sank as she saw that Eugenie Postlethwaite was waiting for him. But still, the sight had come as a timely reminder: she would be unwise to allow herself to entertain feelings towards Alex that could not possibly be returned.

'Thank you,' she said formally. 'That was most enjoyable.'

He frowned at her cool manner, but made a polite rejoinder before she excused herself, greeting Lord Chuffington who had just wandered over to her and accepting his hand for the next dance.

The evening was almost over. Cicely gave a sigh of relief. Although it had been enjoyable, it had also been something of a strain, and she would be glad when she could return to the safety of the Lodge. There were no perplexing feelings there. Everything was straightforward and safe.

She went out on to the terrace. Though late—supper was over—it was not yet completely dark. A dusky light still lingered, enhanced by an almost-full moon and the yellow gaslight that streamed out from the Manor. A number of other people had also taken to the terrace. Among them was Alex.

Cicely was about to draw back when one of the group, Mrs Weston, hailed her.

Realizing she could not slip away unseen she went forward to join the small party.

'. . . take it down altogether,' young Mr Phelps was saying. 'It blocks the view, Evington, you know it does.'

'Perhaps. I might do that,' replied Alex, as he smoked a cigar and swirled a brandy in his glass.

Cicely looked enquiringly at Mrs Weston, wondering what they were talking about.

'The chestnut,' said Mrs Weston.

'Ugly thing, and completely unnecessary,' said Mr Phelps, waving towards a magnificent chestnut which had stood in the centre of the

166

lawns for time out of mind.

Cicely felt her stomach lurch. *Not the chestnut,* she wanted to cry, but she had no right to do so. Alex was entitled to do whatever he wanted with the house and grounds; the Manor belonged to him.

Even so, Cicely could not remain to hear her beloved chestnut tree talked about in that way. It had too many memories for her. Mumbling an inarticulate excuse she ran down the steps of the terrace and on to the wide lawns, away from the chattering group. But she had not gone far when she became aware that there was someone behind her. She began to run more quickly: she knew without looking who that someone was, and she did not feel equal to talking to Alex whilst her emotions were running high. Lifting the hem of her gown with one hand she sped across the lawns. But the sound of footsteps grew louder behind her and she began to fear she would not escape. 'Cicely!'

She ignored his voice and ran on.

'Cicely! Stop!'

She glanced over her shoulder and saw that he was almost upon her. She ran forward again but it was no good. He caught her arm and spun her round.

'Cicely, what is it?' he demanded. 'What's wrong?'

'Nothing,' she said.

'Not nothing,' he returned. 'You're as white

167

as a sheet. And you've been crying.'

'No. You're mistaken.'

He pulled her close, taking her chin in his hand. Turning her face he revealed the remains of her tears, glinting on her lashes in the moonlight.

'Something's upset you.'

'No. I assure you it hasn't.' She spoke sharply, not feeling equal to having a conversation with him until she was in control of herself once more.

'Yes, it has,' he said, matching her sharp tone with one equally harsh, 'and I'm not letting you go until I know what it is.'

'You have no right to keep me here,' she said, shaking her arm free and picking up the hem of her gown once more.

'To hell with rights,' he said, his eyes locking on to her own. Such was the intensity of his gaze that she was held motionless. 'I want to know what made you go pale back on the terrace just now, and you are going to tell me.'

'I am . . .' she began, intending to say *I am not*, but suddenly her feelings got the better of her. 'How can you do it?' she suddenly burst out, no longer able to contain herself.

He looked taken aback. 'How can I do what?' he asked.

She dropped the hem of her gown. 'Cut down the chestnut tree.'

He looked at her uncomprehendingly. 'You're upset about a *tree*?'

'It isn't just a tree,' she said rashly. 'It's the tree my great-great-great-grandmother planted when she was a little girl of three years old. My family have played in it and sheltered under it for over two hundred years, generation upon generation of them. My mother and I hid in it when we played with my father—she lifted me into the branches and then climbed up beside me, whilst my father searched for us high and low, and in the end we had to call to him, or he would never have found us. It was summer, and the leaves were thick,' she said defiantly. Then her face paled again. 'But you wouldn't understand.'

She turned to go. 'You're wrong,' he said.

She was already walking away from him, but his words halted her. She hesitated. Then turned.

His eyes were burning with a strange intensity. 'I do understand,' he said.

She almost believed him. But then she said, with a shuddering sigh, 'No, you don't. You are going to cut it down.'

The air was suddenly still. Not a tree rustled. Not a leaf stirred.

'No.'

'N . . . no?' she asked hesitantly.

'No.'

He shook his head, and the gesture caught the moonlight, which lit the side of his face and painted silver streaks into his hair. 'I'm not going to cut it down.'

169

'But you said . . .' she began.

'That's before I realized what it meant to you.'

There was a light in his velvety eyes that neither she, nor anyone else had ever seen there before.

'You would spare it . . . for me?'

He reached out his hand and pulled her gently into his arms. He stroked a stray tendril away from her face. 'Yes. I would.'

She relaxed against him, and felt him pressing his lips against her hair, then against her forehead. He lifted her chin, and his eyes roamed over her face. Her hands rose of their own volition against the lapels of his dinner jacket. The fabric was warm and soft to the touch. Beneath it, his muscles were firm.

She shuddered, overcome with his nearness. She was unnaturally aware of him: his hair, with one lock falling across his forehead; his eyes, with their fine lines at the corners; and his chin, with its day's growth of beard.

And he was unnaturally aware of her. She could tell by the way his eyes trailed over her body, lingering on the whiteness of her shoulders and the soft curve of her breasts.

He took her face between his hands, and—

'Thief!' The cry cut into the night like a knife. 'Someone has stolen my necklace!'

Cicely's eyes flew open.

'Damn!' Alex cursed under his breath. His eyes held Cicely's as though unable to let them go.

Then, 'Thief!' The cry came again. It could no longer be ignored. Nor could the hubbub coming from the direction of the house as more voices took up the cry.

'I have to go. But you're coming with me,' he said. He took her by the hand and ran towards the Manor, with Cicely running alongside him.

'What is it? What's happened?' he said as, dropping Cicely's hand at the last moment, he strode into the house. He sounded genuinely ignorant, as though he had no idea what had just happened, and as though he had not been expecting a theft.

'My necklace,' said Miss Postlethwaite, playing her part to perfection. 'My beautiful emerald necklace. Someone has stolen it.'

By now, all the guests had assembled in the ballroom, drawn there from the terrace and the supper-room by Miss Postlethwaite's cries. They were busily exclaiming over the theft, and cries of, 'Her necklace!' and 'Those magnificent emeralds!' pierced the night.

'If I could have your attention,' said Alex, taking control. He strode into the middle of the ballroom and addressed his guests. 'It seems that a most unfortunate incident has occurred.' He turned to Miss Postlethwaite. 'You are sure you were wearing your necklace tonight? Forgive me for asking, but it is as well to examine every possibility before we consider

171

theft.'

'Quite sure,' said Miss Postlethwaite.

'And the necklace could not have slipped off?'

'No.' Miss Postlethwaite spoke definitely. Absolutely not.'

'Then, ladies and gentlemen,' said Alex, looking round the company, 'if I might ask you all to remain in the ballroom. Unfortunately I feel it is my duty to call the police, and that being so, I feel sure they will be able to clear up this matter more speedily if we are all in one—'

A rustle of conversation, which had started as a whisper at the back of the room, now found full voice, and someone said, 'The maid. The maid took it.'

All eyes turned to the hapless maid who stood with a trayful of oysters in the middle of the room.

'Who said that?' demanded Alex.

But no one knew where the voice had come from.

'Might as well search her, just to be on the safe side,' said Mrs Yarrow sensibly.

'Go ahead,' said Gladys, the maid. 'I ain't got nothing to hide. Look, all I've got in my apron pocket,' she said, plunging her hand deep into that article of clothing, 'is—' Her face changed, and out of the pocket she drew . . .

'Miss Postlethwaite's necklace.' Mrs

Yarrow's voice broke the silence that had filled the room.

A hubbub of voices broke out.

'I shouldn't stand for it, Evington,' came a voice from the crowd.

'Dismiss her!' came another.

Alex felt himself rapidly becoming caught up in a nightmare. He had no wish to dismiss Gladys, but he knew that unless he did so—or at least appeared to do so—the Honourable Martin Goss would not relax, and there was no telling what he might do if that happened.

Inwardly cursing, Alex said, 'Gladys, you are dismissed. You will wait in my study until the police arrive.'

'But I never . . .' began Gladys, before she realized it would do no good, and her voice tailed off in a sob. 'Yes, sir,' she said brokenly.

'Take over here,' said Alex in an aside to Roddy, as Gladys left the room. 'Soothe everyone's ruffled feathers and get the evening back on an even keel. It's no good: Goss has been too slippery for us—this time.'

'But we will get him?' asked Roddy anxiously.

'Oh, yes.' Alex's voice was steely. 'We'll get him. It's just a matter of time.'

*   *   *

Seething, Cicely followed Gladys from the room. How could Alex have treated the girl so

173

disgracefully? she thought angrily. Following Gladys into the study, she found the poor girl wiping her eyes on her apron and sobbing bitterly.

'Oh, miss, I never took it!' Gladys cried, as Cicely slipped into the study behind her.

'No, of course you didn't,' said Cicely soothingly. 'I never for one moment thought you did.'

'Oh, miss, I'm that relieved,' said Gladys, beginning to sob less violently. 'I thought you suspected me like everyone else and I couldn't bear it. Not after you was kind enough to get me this job at the Manor.' Her face crumpled again. 'But what's going to happen now, miss? I'll never get another job. Mr Evington won't give me a reference, and word of this'll be all round Little Oakleigh, and Greater Oakleigh, too, by tomorrow, if I don't miss my guess, so who will employ me now?'

'Hush, Gladys. Dry your eyes. It is not as bad as you think. If the worst comes to the worst, you can always come and work for me. I have been thinking for some time that I need a maid at the Lodge.'

'Oh, miss, it's that kind of you, but everyone knows how hard it's been for you since your father died. There ain't no way you can afford to take on a maid, not even with your job at the Manor.'

'My job at the Manor?' asked Cicely faintly. She had had no idea anyone else knew about it.

Gladys nodded. 'Yes, miss. You needs what you make from your job to pay Tom to help Gibson.'

'How did you know?' asked Cicely, mystified. 'I thought I had kept my secret so well.'

'Ain't no such thing as a secret,' sniffed Gladys. 'Not in Little Oakleigh.'

Cicely gave a rueful smile. 'I suspect you are right.' The village was a small place, and sooner or later even the best-kept secrets slipped out. 'But don't worry, Gladys, I will help you to find another position. Meanwhile, I intend to speak to Mr Evington on your behalf. Once he realizes that you are not the sort of girl to steal a necklace, I am sure he will relent.'

Gladys looked unconvinced. Nevertheless, her conversation with Cicely had done much to soothe her, and when Cicely said she meant to go and find Mr Evington and speak to him that very minute, Gladys said nothing to detain her.

Straightening her shoulders, Cicely passed out of the room . . . not noticing Alex standing in the shadows in the hallway, stunned.

The conversation he had overheard had shaken him to his foundations. It had made him reconsider all his preconceived notions about Cicely, and acknowledge that he had been completely wrong about her. He had come to Oakleigh Manor prepared—no, if he was honest with himself, he had come to Oakleigh Manor *determined*—to dislike her, and he had attributed to her thoughts and feelings she did not possess. Before he had even met her he had classed her as one of the people who had made life so impossible for his sister, but that was completely false. Far from turning against Gladys, as others had turned against Katie when she had been falsely accused, Cicely had gone out of her way to help the girl. And if Cicely had been present when Katie had needed help, he realized that she would have helped Katie as well.

And just what other preconceived notions had he been clinging to for the past few weeks? he asked himself.

The notion that Cicely's father had been an arrogant and careless man, happy to ruin innocent tradesmen by never paying his bills— that too had been one of his unjustified thoughts. For instead of being an arrogant and careless man who felt himself too grand to settle his accounts, Mr Haringay had instead been a harmless eccentric who had retreated from the world after his beloved wife had died and he had been guilty of nothing worse than absent-mindedness.

Then again, there was the idea that Cicely was a wealthy woman who had taken a job as his secretary out of boredom, when such was not the case. She had taken a job in order to pay the salary of a boy to help her aging butler, as the conversation he had just overheard had revealed.

And what of his idea that she had been glad to get rid of the Manor, seeing it as a white elephant? Her distress at the thought of the chestnut being cut down showed that her feelings were quite otherwise. Far from viewing the Manor as a draughty old barn of a place, as he had assumed, she had loved it as her home, for that was what it had been. To her, it was the house in which she and her family had lived for generation after generation, and it carried with it happy memories of her childhood, and the mother she had lost at an early age.

From beginning to end, Alex realized, he had built his judgements of her, not on fair and just observation as he usually did, but on prejudice.

It was not pleasant, but it must be acknowledged for all that. He had been wilfully blind.

The realization brought other feelings in its wake. Warm feelings for Cicely which he had too long denied . . .

The sound of Gladys sobbing brought him back to the present, and forced him to put his other thoughts aside—for now. Entering the study, he quickly reassured the girl that she would not lose her position.

'I never meant to dismiss you,' he said, 'but I had to say it in order to calm my guests. You have nothing to fear, however. I know you did not take the necklace and you will not suffer for it having been found in your apron.' Then, on a different note, he asked, 'Do you know how it got there, Gladys?'

'No, sir, I'm sure I don't.'

'Did any of the guests bump into you? Might one of them have dropped it in your apron pocket?'

Gladys's face creased in concentration. Then she shook her head. 'I couldn't rightly say, sir.'

'Very well, Gladys. I suggest you go to your room, and we will speak of this again in the morning.'

'Very good, sir.'

Gladys went out, shutting the door behind her.

Leaving Alex to ponder anew the warm and fulfilling emotions that were flooding his breast.

*   *   *

Cicely had looked all over for Alex, but he was nowhere to be found. The orchestra was playing again, she noticed, and people were dancing. She had expected an air of constraint to be hanging over the party, but the opposite had happened. The theft of the necklace had given people something to talk about, and now that the culprit had been found and punished—or so they thought—the guests could enjoy reliving the sensation.

But none of that helped Cicely. She still needed to find Alex and convince him that Gladys had had nothing to do with the theft. But she had the feeling that she knew who had been responsible . . .

At last, being unable to find Alex, she returned to the study in order to tell Gladys that she should go to bed. To her surprise, she found Alex there.

He turned round as she entered the room.

'Come in, and shut the door.'

Cicely did as he said, preparing herself to stand up for Gladys, but his first words told her that would not be necessary.

'You have no need to worry,' he said. 'I know Gladys is innocent.'

She looked at him in surprise. Then asked, 'How?'

'Because,' he said, 'I planned tonight's robbery. Oh, not its execution,' he hastened to reassure her. 'But I planned for it to happen. Miss Postlethwaite is—let's just say, she is a friend of mine—and her necklace was the bait. You see, it is not the first time this has happened, that a valuable piece of jewellery has been stolen at a fashionable gathering—'

'I know.' Cicely sighed, and sat down. And I believe I know who the culprit is.'

It was his turn to look surprised. 'You do?'

She nodded. 'I can't prove it, unfortunately,

but I believe the thief is the Honourable Martin Goss.'

She saw the blank look of astonishment on his face. Misunderstanding his expression, and thinking that he was astonished at the fact she had accused an honourable gentleman of being a thief, instead of realizing that he was astonished that she knew the thief's identity, she went on to explain.

'A few years ago, I had a Season in London, thanks to the generosity of one of my aunts. I went to stay with her, and we attended many balls and soirées. At one of the soirées a valuable brooch was stolen. It was never recovered. But just before it disappeared I had seen the Honourable Goss bump into the lady who owned it. The next second it had vanished.'

'The next second, you say?'

'Yes. You see, I had just been looking at the brooch, and admiring it from a distance. Then Martin Goss bumped into the lady and, when he had excused himself, her brooch was no longer there.'

'And you think he took it?'

'I am certain of it.'

'And so am I.'

Briefly, he explained about the theft that had occurred whilst Katie had been in service, and the conclusion of the painful episode.

'I see.' Cicely let out a long sigh. 'So that is why you dislike the landed gentry, because

180

they treated your sister unfairly, and cast her off without any means of support. No wonder you were so hostile when you came here.'

'I was wrong to be so. I was judging you on something you had had no part in.' He gave a wry smile. 'My only consolation is that you also judged me.'

She said ruefully, 'You're right. I did.'

'Is it really so terrible?' he asked, suddenly serious. 'My being a cit?' His eyes scanned her face, as though he would find the answer written there.

She swallowed. 'It isn't terrible at all.'

A wave of relief washed over his face. Breaking the tension that was rapidly gathering he said with a smile, 'But you didn't like me. Admit it. You were as prejudiced against me to begin with as I was against you.'

Cicely shook her head. 'No. I wasn't prejudiced. Or, at least, it wasn't entirely prejudice. It's true I didn't have a high opinion of cits—they have no idea of how to behave in the countryside—but my dislike of you wasn't based on something someone else had done. I disliked you because of what you yourself had done—or rather, not done.'

He looked at her enquiringly.

'I disliked you because you didn't come to look at the Manor. Everyone else came to look. They commented on its grandeur, and its picturesqueness, and its lovely views. But you bought it as though it was something of no consequence. You didn't even bother to come to look at it yourself, and that hurt me: you sent your agent to look at it instead. You didn't value the Manor as I wanted you to. It wasn't, to you, a home; it was nothing but an investment.'

He let out a long sigh. 'What you say is true, up to a point—but only up to a point. The reason I didn't come to look at the Manor was because I never meant to settle here. I simply needed a grand house in which to set the stage for another robbery to take place. That being the case, one house was as good as another.'

Her spirits lifted as she realized he was not the insensitive person she had supposed. But then they quickly sank again as she took in the full implication of his words. 'Then . . . you don't intend to settle here?' she asked. Her voice sounded hollow to her own ears. 'You will be going back to London once you have caught the thief?'

And why did that thought make her stomach clench? she wondered.

But before Alex could answer her, the door opened and Roddy entered the room.

Cicely stepped away from Alex, immediately brought back to her senses. She was in a small room far from the main body of the company with a gentleman. If word of it got out, it would give rise to gossip of a malicious kind, and although she was too well liked in the neighbourhood for it to do her any real harm,

182

still it was something she would rather avoid.

'I must go,' she said.

She suited her actions to her words and slipped out of the room.

'Sorry,' said Roddy sheepishly.

'Your timing is atrocious,' said Alex, trying to make the remark humorous, but with an edge of tension in his voice.

'It's just that your guests seem about ready to leave.'

Alex nodded. 'I'll join you in a minute,' he said.

Roddy left, and after straightening his bow tie Alex followed him out of the room.

Only to bump into Lord Chuffington.

'I say,' said Chuff Chuff, 'have you seen my fiancée anywhere?'

'I didn't know you had a fiancée,' remarked Alex.

'Good lord, yes. Had one for ever.'

'Congratulations,' said Alex, keen to make up for his earlier unjustified resentment against the landed classes by being particularly affable to Lord Chuffington. 'And when is the wedding to be?'

'Oh, soon,' said Chuff Chuff amiably. 'Not easy—funerals and what not—but all that's over with now. Dare say it will be any time now.'

'I wish you every happiness,' said Alex. 'As to having seen your fiancée, I won't know whether I've seen her or not until you tell me who she is.'

'What? Oh, yes, it's Cicely. Cicely Haringay.'

Alex felt every limb grow still. 'Cicely Haringay?' he repeated.

'Yes. You know. Used to own the Manor. Lives down at the Lodge. Moving to Parmiston soon, though, of course. Wouldn't want to live at the Lodge for ever.'

'No.' Alex's voice was hollow. 'I don't suppose she would.'

'Used to better things,' said Chuff Chuff.

Alex forced the words out. 'As you say. She's used to better things.' Then, rousing himself, he said, 'No. I'm sorry, Chuffington, I don't know where she is.'

'Oh, well. Better cut along then.'

And so saying he ambled off in search of Cicely, leaving Alex feeling as though Chuffington had struck him a body blow. Chuffington? Engaged to Cicely? It couldn't be.

But why couldn't it be? They were two of a kind. Both from the landed classes and both from the same neighbourhood, it was just the sort of marriage that was taking place all the time.

Cursing himself for having thought . . . but never mind what he'd thought. He'd been a fool. Cicely was engaged to Chuffington. He refused to recognize the hollow emptiness that swept over him, or acknowledge what it meant.

184

Cicely was to marry Lord Chuffington. And that was the end of it.

*   *   *

'We failed.'

Eugenie sounded as tired as Alex felt. He had just said farewell to the last of the guests who had spent the evening at the Manor for the ball, whilst his house guests had retired upstairs to bed. Now Eugenie and Alex, together with Roddy, were sitting in the drawing-room discussing their failed attempt to catch Goss.

'I know.'

'It was my fault. I should have checked to see that Gladys hadn't come back into the room before I raised the alarm,' she said.

'That wasn't your job,' said Roddy morosely. 'It was my job to make sure there were no maids present, so that Goss couldn't frame another innocent young girl, and then give you a sign so that you could cry thief. And that's what you did.'

'It was no one's fault,' said Alex. 'We couldn't have foreseen that Gladys would slip back into the room at such a critical moment.'

'Why *did* she return?' asked Roddy curiously. 'Have you asked her?'

Alex nodded. 'It was because she found Mrs Godiver's handkerchief. Mrs Godiver had dropped it in the hallway and Gladys

185

recognized it, so she was going to return it.'

'Unluckily for us,' said Eugenie. 'Because Goss took advantage of the situation and put the necklace in her apron pocket. He's an even more accomplished thief than we thought.'

'I wish we could have caught him,' sighed Roddy.

'But we didn't,' said Eugenie despondently.

'We will,' said Alex. 'We'll just have to come up with a better plan—one in which he will have no opportunity to slip the stolen article into the pocket of an innocent maid.'

'It's no good,' said Roddy, thrusting his hands deep into his pockets and scowling at the carpet. 'He won't come here again.'

'Cheer up.' Alex did his best to sound confident, although he was far from feeling it. 'We'll think of something. But we'll do it better after a good night's sleep.'

'You're right,' said Eugenie, standing up. 'Still, there is one good thing. We might not have caught Goss, but at least we didn't lose the necklace. It would have been the last straw if he'd managed to evade capture and got away with the jewels as well.'

'Although—' Although then we would have had a chance of catching him when he tried to dispose of them, Alex had been about to say. But he thought better of it. Eugenie's remark had lifted both hers and Roddy's spirits, and Alex did not want to cast them down again.

Roddy looked at him enquiringly.

Alex shook his head. 'Oh, nothing,' he said. 'It's late. We're all tired. I suggest we leave any further discussion until the morning.'

Eugenie and Roddy, worn out by the night's events, agreed.

'Time for bed,' said Eugenie, yawning. She stood up. 'Good night, Alex.'

Alex bade her and Roddy goodnight, but when they went upstairs he did not go with them. Instead, he lingered in the drawing-room. It was no use him going to bed; he knew he would not sleep . . . because Cicely was engaged to Lord Chuffington. Try as he might to get it out of his head he couldn't do it. It was on his mind the whole time. Despite all rational thoughts to the contrary, he still could not believe it. But why not? As Chuffington said, she was used to living in a manor house. No more living in a lodge. No more faulty ranges. And no more having to work as a secretary in order to make ends meet.

But it seemed so unlike Cicely.

Fool! he told himself angrily as he strode over to the fireplace and stood looking down into the empty grate. You're doing it again. Investing her with qualities she doesn't have. First, you convinced yourself she was an upper-class termagant who would have dismissed Katie for something she didn't do—which was completely wide of the mark. Now, you're trying to convince yourself she wouldn't marry for a position in society—and again you're completely wrong. You're trying to give her feelings she does not possess.

What was it about Cicely that provoked such strong reactions in him, he wondered? Why should he care if she married? Or who she married? He had never been interested in young women before—in a casual way, yes, or in a brotherly way, like with Katie, or a friendly way, like with Eugenie, but never in this distracted way, seeing things that simply weren't there. If she wanted to marry Chuffington, why should it bother him? And not just bother him, cut him into little pieces?

He strode across the room and stood looking out over the lawns. What Cicely did with her life was up to her, he told himself. There was nothing between them but an electric physical attraction—and yet in all honesty he had to acknowledge that for him it was more than that. The feelings which had been churning round in him for some time now were becoming clearer . . . but he must get over them. Cicely had made her choice. So all he had to do now was forget her.

Yes. That was all . . .

The door opened, breaking in on his thoughts. He looked round, and there was Cicely. Standing in the doorway, with the gas light from the hallway casting a golden halo round her, she looked more lovely than he had ever seen her. Her ash-blonde hair was soft and inviting, her slight curves appealing in

188

her fashionably low-cut gown. Her skin was golden, and her eyes were full of beauty.

'You can't do it,' he said.

He shouldn't have said it, but he couldn't let her throw herself away on Chuffington.

Her lips parted in surprise.

He couldn't take his eyes away from them. She had the most kissable lips he had ever seen. And how he longed to kiss them again.

She seemed to know exactly what he was talking about. 'It will work,' she said.

It will work. Could she really believe that? he asked himself.

'But how did you know?' she queried.

His voice was tight. He made an effort to make it sound normal. 'It was Chuffington. He told me.'

She looked perplexed. 'But Chuff Chuff doesn't know. I haven't told him about my plan.'

'Plan?' Alex frowned. How could marriage be a plan? Unless they were at cross purposes. 'What plan?' he asked cautiously.

'My plan for catching Martin Goss.'

Her words stunned him. Her plan for catching Martin Goss?

And then he was out of the strange state that had gripped him when he had seen her enter the room, and back in the real world. He gave a sigh, though whether it was of frustration or relief he didn't know. He had been about to tell her that she couldn't marry

Chuffington; to sweep her into his arms and prove it to her with hot words and impassioned kisses; but her unexpected words had brought him back down to earth.

'I can't be sure, of course,' she said. 'Perhaps I should have said, I *think* it will work.'

'Come in,' he said belatedly. 'Have a seat. I was surprised to see you,' he said by way of explanation of his strange behaviour. 'I thought all the houseguests had gone to bed.'

'They have. But I wanted to speak to you, and I did not want to leave it until tomorrow, so I stayed behind. I have already seen two innocent young women blamed for Martin Goss's crimes, and I don't want to see it happen again. I won't rest until he has been put behind bars.'

His surprise quickly gave way to understanding. 'I feel the same. Unfortunately, I don't see what else I can do,' he said, sitting down opposite her. 'Goss will not attend another party given at the Manor, nor, I suspect, any other party given by me. I haven't given up hope of bringing him to justice, but at the moment I cannot see a way to do it.'

'But I can.'

He looked at her with interest. 'Go on.'

Cicely took a deep breath, and then began. 'According to Gibson, who hears all the local servants' gossip, Martin Goss is badly in need of money, and I believe he will soon strike again. He is deeply in debt and needs to get out of it as quickly as possible. It is my belief he will attempt to steal something of significant value when he goes to Marienbad.'

'Marienbad?' Alex raised his eyebrows. He did not know the name of the town.

'It's in Austria, a spa town,' she explained. 'It's funny, the more things change the more they stay the same—my great-grandmother used to take the waters at the start of the last century, in Bath, and now people go to Marienbad to do the same thing. Society still likes to take the waters as much as it has always done, only now it takes them abroad instead of at home. Marienbad attracts all the best people. King Edward himself is a regular visitor.'

'And you think Goss is likely to go there?' he asked.

'I know he is. Mrs Capstone was complaining about it only last week. "We are going to Marienbad at the end of August", she said. "As you know, we go every year. I do so enjoy it, and I'm convinced it does Herbert's bronchitis good. My only regret is that the wretched Martin Goss will be there. His mother is the most charming of women, but Martin is a cad". So you see, I know he is going.'

Alex's eyes became alert. He pushed himself out of his chair and strode over to the fireplace. 'It has possibilities,' he said, turning the idea over in his mind. 'Distinct possibilities. Once out of England, Goss might well grow careless. It's worth a try.' He drummed his fingers on the marble mantelpiece. 'But I don't see how we are to know where and when he will strike.'

'I have already thought about that. We will have to lay another trap.'

Alex looked at her searchingly. 'I don't see how we can do it. He won't come to another of my parties, and I doubt if he will come to one of yours. We were both present when Eugenie's necklace was taken, and it will be too risky for him to carry out another theft if we are there.'

'That is not what I was thinking of.'

He looked at her enquiringly.

Taking a deep breath, Cicely began to outline her idea.

Alex's eyes grew admiring as her plan unfolded. 'It might work,' he said. 'Yes, it just might.' Then his eyes became penetrating. 'But are you sure your cousin will help us?'

'Positive. Sophie is an accomplished actress—if her mother would let her, she would go on the stage! She will relish the opportunity of playing a part.'

'Then we'll give it a try. But we will have to be careful. We must make sure Goss does not see us in Marienbad. If he does, he might not take the bait. Which means we will have to stay elsewhere.'

'I will be staying with my Aunt Hilda in her villa on the outskirts of Marienbad, as I have already explained to you, and I suggest you stay at the neighbouring town of Karlsbad. The Hotel Savoy has a good reputation, and you should be comfortable there. That way, we will be able to escape Goss's notice and he will not see us until it is too late—if indeed he sees us at all, which, if all goes to plan, he won't.'

'And when is he going to Marienbad?' asked Alex. 'Do you know?'

'Yes. He will be going within the next few weeks.'

Alex nodded. 'Then I suggest we get there as soon as possible, so that we can lay our plans.'

Cicely agreed. 'I will write to my aunt straight away, so that she will be expecting me.' She stood up. 'But now, it is late.'

He stood as well.

'I will bid you goodnight,' she said.

He fought down an urge to stop her, and she walked out of the room.

CHAPTER EIGHT

The house party broke up amongst cries of thanks the following day, and Cicely, taking her leave of Alex with Alice and Mrs Babbage at her elbow, added her own to the general clamour.

'Yes, indeed, thank you so much for having us, Mr Evington,' said Mrs Babbage, joining her thanks to Cicely and Alice's. 'We have had a wonderful time.'

'I'm glad you enjoyed it,' said Alex.

He was all that was polite and urbane, but Cicely couldn't help missing the intimacy of the previous day. There was nothing left of it now, however. It had entirely gone, and no matter what her feelings were for him she had to face the fact that his feelings for her were not of the same kind. Whilst he might sympathize with her over the destruction of something that was dear to her—for there had been no mistaking the look of tenderness in his eyes when he had promised her not to cut down the chestnut tree—it was obvious that that was as far as his gentler feelings went. He clearly had an intimate relationship with Eugenie Postlethwaite, and Cicely told herself that, although he might be increasingly important to her—far more important than was wise—she must remember that she meant nothing to him. To him, she was simply the young woman from whom he had bought his house: a house he did not even intend to live in, once he had fulfilled his purpose of bringing the Honourable Martin Goss to justice.

Which was probably just as well, she thought, with a sudden weariness. Because for some reason she did not dare examine, it would break her heart to see him living there with Eugenie Postlethwaite as his wife.

'Well, that was most enjoyable,' said Mrs Babbage, recalling Cicely to the present. She gave a sigh of satisfaction and the three ladies, having taken their leave of their host, began to walk down the road to the Lodge. 'And how kind it was of Mr Evington to send our luggage home for us by motor car. He really is a most agreeable man.'

Talk of Alex's virtues did nothing to help Cicely put Alex out of her mind, and she was grateful therefore when they reached the door of the Lodge.

'You are sure you will not come and stay with us for a few days?' asked Mrs Babbage.

'No, thank you, it really isn't necessary,' said Cicely. 'The repairs have gone well, and the Lodge is habitable again.'

'Then in that case, I will bid you farewell.'

Cicely and Alice took an affectionate leave of each other, and then Cicely went into the Lodge. After the turmoil of the previous week she was looking forward to a little peace and quiet before leaving the Lodge again, this time for Marienbad, in order to catch Martin Goss.

But before then she had plenty to do. Peace and quiet did not mean inactivity, and she set about checking the kitchen thoroughly to make sure that it had been properly repaired—although she had paid one or two visits to the Lodge during the week, it was only now that she was home again that could she give it the scrutiny it really needed. To her relief she saw that, apart from the fact that the kitchen now lacked a range, the room was as good as new. The hole in the wall had been closed up, and only a slight difference in the colour of the paintwork showed that a repair had taken place. Which left her with only one problem: the lack of a range. She sighed. She would have to have one sooner or later, as she could not possibly manage without one. The range provided all the hot water, as well as all the cooking facilities, for the Lodge, and although she could do without such things in summer, by the time the winter came she would be needing them. She felt her spirits sink. Every time she was getting her head above water some new disaster took place.

Ah well! she thought bracingly, she would just have to find a way of solving this problem as she had found a way of solving all her others. And fortunately she had several months in which to do it. By the time winter came, something would no doubt turn up. In the meantime she had her visit to Marienbad to occupy her mind . . . for which she must begin to make her arrangements.

* * *

Cicely felt her excitement mount as the steam

train pulled into Marienbad station. It was three years since she had last visited the spa town, and she was looking forward to seeing her aunt and cousin again.

How fortunate she was to have such a generous aunt, she thought, as the puffing and blowing train ground to a halt. Not only had Aunt Hilda made her welcome whenever she had visited, but had always insisted on paying her fares. Without this generosity, Cicely knew she would never have been able to visit.

And there was Aunt Hilda now!

Cicely waved at her aunt, who was standing on the platform beside Cousin Sophie. Her aunt, seeing her, raised her hand in greeting, and Sophie waved wildly, full of the exuberance of youth.

Mrs Lessing was looking exactly the same as the last time she had seen her, thought Cicely as she stepped off the train, being a fine-looking woman in her forties. Her mouse-brown hair was pulled back from her face and arranged in a simple knot at the back of her head. Her slim figure—the product of vigorous walks through the surrounding pine forests, which even now were perfuming the air with their fresh, clean scent—was encased in a high-necked blouse, a long skirt and a tailored jacket. Ever practical, she carried an umbrella, which was often needed in Marienbad, whatever the time of year.

Sophie, in contrast, was looking completely

different to the last time Cicely had seen her. The three intervening years had brought about a definite change. Gone was the gawky fifteen-year-old schoolgirl, and in her place was a beautiful young woman with elegantly coiffured golden curls and the most immaculate clothes. Her promenade dress was definitely Parisian—probably, thought Cicely, a creation of Maison Worth—and had an unmistakable air of chic. Setting it off was a plumed hat that was perched most becomingly on the back of her pretty young head. But for all her cousin's new-found maturity, Cicely was pleased to see that she still had a mischievous sparkle in her eye, for without it the plan to catch Goss could not go ahead.

'Cicely.' Her aunt greeted her affectionately, kissing her on both cheeks. 'It is lovely to have you here.'

'It's lovely to be here. I'd forgotten how beautiful Marienbad is,' she said, looking round at the pine forests which could be seen rising all round the town and stretching off into the distance.

'You must have plenty of walks now you are here. You are looking a little peaky,' said her aunt, surveying her closely. She gave a sigh. 'But then, after your father's death, it is not to be wondered at.'

'Cicely!' Sophie could not contain herself any longer. 'It seems like an age since I last saw you. I am so glad you are here. And in such mysterious circumstances. Your letter said everything and nothing. What sort of help do you need? It all sounds very exciting.'

Cicely laughed at Sophie's enthusiasm. 'I will tell you all about it . . . but not on the station platform.'

'Oh, no, of course not. We have to get a taxi to the villa, as we don't have a motor car,' she said, as a porter took Cicely's luggage and loaded it on to a hand cart. 'I keep trying to persuade mother to let me learn to drive but she says it isn't suitable.' Sophie gave a mischievous smile and glanced sideways at her mother. 'It seems to me that nothing interesting ever is.'

'You, miss, are becoming fast,' said Cicely's aunt reprovingly. 'Your father would turn in his grave.'

Cicely's Uncle Harry had died some years before, in Marienbad, where the family had originally moved for the good of his health. It had been a wise idea, and had worked well for a time, as his health had shown a distinct improvement, but unfortunately he had then succumbed to a bad bout of pneumonia and had sadly died. His wife and daughter, however, had continued to live in Marienbad, where they had made many friends.

'Have I changed since you saw me last?' asked Sophie, as the three of them went out of the station and hailed a taxi.

'Completely. You were a girl when I saw you

last. Now you're a young woman.'

Sophie was pleased to hear this, and together the three of them climbed into the taxi. Once Cicely's luggage had been loaded they drove through the pine forests to the villa, which was on the outskirts of the town. It was a large house, with a long veranda running along the front. Pleasant gardens surrounded it, and beyond them lay the forest.

'You will want to refresh yourself,' said her aunt, as she showed Cicely up to her room. 'Come down when you are ready. You know the way.'

Cicely smiled. The villa was almost as familiar to her as the Manor or the Lodge, and she did indeed know her way around.

Once her aunt had gone she threw open the window of her bedroom and breathed in deeply, savouring the delicious scent of pine. She looked out over the tree-clad slopes and down on to the town in order to reacquaint herself with her surroundings. She could make out the Kirchenplatz, the famous square in which the Hotel Weimar stood, and by standing on tiptoe she could just see the hotel itself. Being late August, she knew the king would be in residence, and she imagined him in his personal suite, reading his newspaper or taking a glass of the health-giving waters for which the town was famous. It was strange to think of being so close to her king. She might even see him, if she was lucky, on one of his frequent strolls.

Turning away from the window she washed and changed. She put on a long mauve skirt and a lace-trimmed blouse that her aunt's maid had by now unpacked, then she went downstairs. Her aunt and cousin were there, reading the newspaper.

'Good. You're here. I'll ring for coffee,' said Mrs Lessing. She paused before pulling the bell. 'That is, if you wouldn't rather have tea? Though I wouldn't if I were you. It is no better than the last time you were here. It's the water—it simply doesn't seem to make good tea. But it makes delicious coffee.'

'Yes, coffee, thank you,' said Cicely.

The servants were efficient, and before long a silver coffee pot was set before Mrs Lessing, complete with sugar and cream. Mrs Lessing poured, and Cicely sipped it thankfully: after her journey, she was in need of something sweet and hot.

'It was good of you to have me, Aunt. Especially at such notice,' she said as she embarked on her second cup of coffee.

'Nonsense. We are delighted to have you. You have livened up our summer. We are very quiet as a rule, and it is good to have a little excitement from time to time.'

'I can't wait to hear all about it,' said Sophie. 'Your letter was very mysterious. Why do you need my help? Though I am very glad you do—it will be so nice to be useful, for a change. Life here is very pleasant, but it is very dull. What is it exactly that you want me to do?'

'Let Cicely finish her coffee in peace!' Mrs Lessing remonstrated with her daughter.

Sophie sighed. 'Very well.' She turned to Cicely. 'But as soon as you have finished I want to know all about it.'

'As to that,' said Cicely, as she put down her cup, 'you will have to wait a little longer. I still have one or two details that I need to work out. But I can tell you something: there has been a robbery at the Manor—'

'A robbery?' asked Sophie, her eyes shining: she was young enough to see only the excitement of the situation, and none of the possible perils.

'Nothing of value, I hope?' asked Mrs Lessing, with a frown.

'No. In fact, the robbery was foiled. But it could have been very serious.' Cicely explained about the attempt to steal Miss Postlethwaite's necklace.

'That is very unfortunate,' said Mrs Lessing, 'but quite frankly, Cicely, I don't see what it has to do with you.'

Cicely went on to explain that the attempt had been perpetrated by Martin Goss, who had evaded capture by slipping the necklace into Gladys's apron and thereby implicating the girl.

'Not Gladys Vicars?' asked Mrs Lessing,

startled.

'Yes.'

Mrs Lessing's brow darkened, for she had visited the Manor on a number of occasions and knew Gladys and her family to be decent people. 'Gladys Vicars is a hardworking, good sort of girl. Martin Goss is a blackguard for doing such a thing—he had no business blaming someone else for his crime, and especially not Gladys, who is such a respectable girl.' Her lips pressed together in a firm line. 'You were right to get involved, Cicely. We can't let men like Martin Goss behave in such a scandalous fashion towards girls like Gladys. Where would it end? We must see to it that he never has an opportunity to do something like this again. There is only one place for him, and that is behind bars.'

'And that is where we intend to put him.'

'We?'

There was a pause. Then Cicely said, as nonchalantly as possible, 'Mr Evington and myself. We are working on the matter together.'

Mrs Lessing gave Cicely a penetrating look. 'Mr Evington is the new owner of the Manor?' she asked.

Cicely flushed—much to her annoyance, for her aunt was a perceptive woman and sometimes saw more than was convenient. 'Yes.'

'I see. He is young?' asked Mrs Lessing.

'Not especially.' Cicely felt awkward, although there was no reason why she should do. Her aunt's questions were innocent enough, and besides, as Cicely wanted her aunt—and her cousin's—help in the matter, it was only right that they should know about the man they would be helping.

'How old is *not especially*?' asked Sophie with interest.

'He is about thirty,' said Cicely, raising her eyes, and looking frankly at her aunt. Fortunately her flush had subsided, and she was once more in control of herself.

'Is he married?' asked Sophie.

Cicely felt in danger of flushing again. 'No. Though I believe he has an . . . attachment.'

'What a pity,' said Sophie. 'I am in need of a husband, and living at the Manor would be just the thing.'

'You are in need of nothing of the sort,' snorted her mother. 'You are far too young to be married. It is hardly any time since you put up your hair and put down your skirts. Mr Evington is far too old for you.' She gave Cicely another penetrating glance, and the words 'but not for you,' hung unspoken in the air. 'However, his private life is not our concern—except as it influences the present situation, that is.' She relaxed her gaze. 'You have told us that he is to be involved in this venture,' she said to Cicely, 'but not why.'

'Because this is not the first time Goss has

stolen—or attempted—to steal something,' said Cicely 'He has done it before, and incriminated another innocent maid. That maid was Katie, Mr Evington's sister.'

'His sister is a maid?' asked Mrs Lessing, startled.

'*Was* a maid,' Cicely corrected her. 'Mr Evington has only recently made his money, in the city, and one of the first things he did was to rescue his sister from service.'

'Family loyalty,' said Mrs Lessing, nodding in appreciation of this side of the situation. 'An estimable quality. Undervalued by the young, but not to be taken lightly nonetheless.' She was thoughtful. 'So Mr Evington has a personal interest in catching Goss.'

'Yes. He has been very helpful with the practical aspects of the plan. In fact, I would not be able to carry it out without him.'

'And the plan is . . . ?' asked Sophie.

Cicely sighed. The strains of the journey were catching up with her. Still, she must tell her aunt and cousin what she would like them to do. She had not explained in her letter, preferring to speak to them face to face.

But before she could speak, Mrs Lessing said, 'You look tired, Cicely. You are in need of a rest. Whatever your plan is, it can wait until morning.'

'Morning?' exclaimed Sophie. 'Oh, no! I will not be able to sleep for wondering about it.'

'In the morning,' said Mrs Lessing firmly.

The clock struck the quarter-hour. 'It is almost time for dinner. And after that, Cicely, I suggest you have an early night. You will need your wits about you tomorrow, from all I have heard.' She turned to Sophie. 'And so will you, my dear.'

*   *   *

The following morning the three ladies rose early, and after a breakfast of coffee and hot rolls they set out for the café where Cicely had already arranged to meet Mr Evington. She had decided, in the end, not to explain her plan over breakfast, thinking it better to wait until Alex was present so that if she forgot anything he would be able to remind her of it. After many grumbles, Sophie had at last given her some peace, resigning herself to the fact that she would have to wait another hour until she found out the part she was expected to play.

Marienbad, unlike many fashionable places at half past nine in the morning, was already busy. The guests, who were there for the good of their health, rose early, taking the waters of the *Kreuzbrunnen* before walking on the promenade. The delightful sound of splashing fountains could be heard, and the cheerful strains of a band.

'I'd forgotten how lovely it is here,' said Cicely appreciatively as they strolled along the

206

promenade.

Suddenly she gave a gasp. A distinguished gentleman was walking towards them, flanked by two other gentlemen. Although there was nothing unusual in his dress, which consisted of a dark-blue coat, white trousers and a grey felt hat, there was something in his carriage that commanded attention. One glance at his noble face, with its fine eyes, dark moustache and distinctive white beard, told Cicely that she was in the presence of her king. Yet there was nothing ostentatious about him; no pomp and circumstance. He was strolling along the promenade in the most natural way.

'Ah.' You've seen him,' said Cicely's aunt.

Cicely tried not to show that she was awe-struck, and forced herself to walk along unconcernedly, but as they reached the king and he wished her aunt a polite 'How do you do?' she could not help feeling delighted. Even better, he addressed a few words to her, asking her how she was enjoying her visit to Marienbad, before strolling on again.

'I had hoped I might meet him, but I didn't really think I would,' said Cicely. 'I did not see him on any of my previous visits.'

'He did not used to come here so often,' said Mrs Lessing. 'But now he comes every year. He is a familiar sight, strolling along the promenade, and he always says a few words in the politest way. He likes to be incognito, as far as possible, when he is here, and does not even use his title, but he is unmistakable nonetheless.'

'No, he doesn't like to use his title,' said Sophie naughtily, 'but that doesn't mean he travels as a nobody. He uses another title instead! He is not King Edward when he is here, but the Duke of Lancaster.'

Mrs Lessing looked at her daughter reprovingly. 'The king is a very busy man, and he is entitled to call himself anything he likes. His visits to Marienbad offer him a brief respite from the pressures of his position, and as to calling himself the Duke of Lancaster, I dare say being a mere duke is as close to being like a normal, everyday person as he will ever get.'

They continued talking about their encounter with King Edward as they made their way to the far end of the promenade, where Alex was waiting for them just outside the café. Cicely's pulse began to beat more quickly at the sight of him, all thoughts of her meeting with King Edward driven from her mind. But she made sure that her inner turmoil did not show on her face. It was unfortunate they had been thrown together by their desire to catch Martin Goss, as it brought to the surface the very feelings she had been trying to suppress, but nevertheless it must be endured.

When they had joined Mr Evington, Cicely performed the introductions. After greeting each other politely the four of them strolled to a nearby café, where they sat at a table that was set apart from the others, as they did not want their conversation to be overheard. They ordered coffee and talked inconsequentially until it arrived, but once the waiter had withdrawn, Sophie said, 'Now, Cicely, I am absolutely bursting to know. Tell us, how are we going to catch the thief?'

Cicely took a sip of the hot coffee then turned to Alex. 'I will rely on you to remind me if I forget anything.'

He nodded. His face caught the shadows from a nearby tree, throwing his features into relief They were strong features, full of character. His wide forehead, arched brows, firm chin and full mouth—determinedly she turned her attention away from his face. It reminded her too much of the way he had kissed her at the Manor. She took a moment to calm her rapidly beating pulse and then began.

'You know that we are hoping to trap Martin Goss,' she said, 'and that Mr Evington is going to help us to do it.' She paused for a moment to gather her thoughts and then continued, 'You also know that Mr Evington has already made an attempt to do so. Unfortunately it failed—for two reasons. One, because as soon as the necklace was taken it was obviously a case of theft, which meant that Martin Goss had to get rid of it as soon as

Miss Postlethwaite cried, "Thief": he could not afford to be found with the necklace on him or else he would have been arrested. And two, because he had a ready-made scapegoat nearby in the form of an innocent maid, which meant that he could dispose of the necklace as soon as it became too dangerous for him to be caught with it.'

'We know that already,' said Sophie impatiently, earning herself a reproving glance from her mother.

Cicely nodded. 'Very well. My plan, then, is once again to tempt him—this time with a valuable tiara—but to do it in such a way that he will feel completely safe about taking it, because it will not appear to have been stolen.'

'But how are you going to do that?' demanded Mrs Lessing. 'Whatever he takes, it will of course appear to have been stolen, because it will have been. And if he becomes alarmed he will plant it on some innocent bystander, just as he did at the Manor. If no maid is available, he will simply choose some other victim to take her place.'

'No. Because, you see, I have come up with a plan which will make sure he has a good reason for taking the tiara, so that it will not seem to be a case of theft even if he is discovered with it in his pocket. That way he will not become alarmed, and we should be able to catch him,' said Cicely.

She caught Alex's eye, and saw the twinkle

there as he noted that Sophie and her mother were looking perplexed, as he had done when he had first heard Cicely outlining her plan.

'It's an ingenious plan,' he assured them.

'I would have put it into effect myself,' went on Cicely, 'but it isn't possible for me to do so as Goss has already seen me, and if I play the lead part in the charade he will know it is a trap.'

'But what *is* the trap?' asked Sophie impatiently.

Cicely turned to her candidly. 'You.'

'Me?' Sophie almost dropped her coffee cup in surprise.

'Yes, you.'

Alex spoke to Cicely. 'I think you had better start at the beginning.'

Cicely nodded. 'You're right. Very well.' She took a deep breath, then she turned to her aunt and said, 'To begin with, I need you to invite Goss to a dinner party at the Kurhaus, because that is where the theft is to take place.'

'But my dear Cicely, why not at our villa?' her aunt interrupted. 'It would be so much easier and more convenient for me to organize a dinner party there.'

'Because there will be too many chances of us losing Goss if we do that. Your villa is on the outskirts of town, and if he steals the tiara there we will have no way of knowing how he will dispose of it: his options will be too wide.

But if the dinner is held at the Kurhaus we believe we know where he will go.'

'I have made some enquiries, and discovered the name of a man who lives close to the Kurhaus.' Alex took over. 'The man buys stolen property, particularly jewellery, at any time of the day or night, with no questions asked.'

'Goss will almost certainly go to him when he has taken the tiara. If our information is correct, he has used this man before. Then, as soon as the transaction takes place, we will have him,' finished Cicely.

'Of course!' exclaimed Sophie, wide-eyed with excitement. 'It's like something out of Sherlock Holmes!' She was delighted with the scheme, for she loved the great detective as much as Cicely did and read all of Arthur Conan Doyle's stories with great enjoyment. 'But you still haven't explained how I come into it, or how the theft is not to seem like theft,' she said.

'You come into it in the most important of ways,' said Cicely. 'You are going to wear the tiara. In short, you are to be our lovely dupe.'

Sophie's eyebrows raised, then she became thoughtful. 'I like that.' Her face took on a slightly silly expression as, born actress that she was, she began to imagine herself into the role. 'But what exactly do I have to do?'

'You have to enchant him,' said Alex with a twinkle.

Cicely elaborated. 'Follow him round the room with your eyes, giggle coquettishly when he speaks to you—' she began.

'No.' Mrs Lessing was firm. 'I will not have a daughter of mine behaving in such a way.'

'But, Mother, it is only a game,' said Sophie.

'One which half of Marienbad will see,' retorted her mother.

'Not if I am discreet.' Sophie leant towards her mother and placed a pleading hand on her arm. 'I promise I will only flirt with him when no one else is watching me, if you are concerned. It is all in a good cause.'

'As to that,' said her mother, 'I don't see how flirting with Martin Goss is going to make him steal your tiara.' She looked at Cicely. 'What has Sophie's behaviour to do with anything?'

'I am just coming to that,' said Cicely. 'After dinner, Sophie, having first flattered him with her obvious adoration, and then impressed him with how silly she is, as well as having given him plenty of opportunity to see what a valuable tiara she is wearing, will engage him in conversation. She will then claim she is overheated.' She turned to Sophie. 'It will be better if you let him suggest a walk, but if not, you are to gaze longingly out of the window and remark on the pleasures of moonlit strolls.'

'Oh, yes, Cicely. How clever!' said Sophie, beginning to see how the plan would work.

213

'He will offer to take you outside and once the two of you are alone you must pretend to swoon. Now this is the difficult part, and will require practice. As you swoon, your tiara must fall from your head.'

Sophie looked surprised, but then said thoughtfully, 'It shouldn't be too difficult. Not if I practise first. And I suppose if it won't come off, I can always raise my hand to my overheated brow and knock it off—discreetly, of course.'

Cicely nodded. 'Once you come out of your swoon,' she continued, 'you are to ask him to escort you to a nearby bench. When he deposits you there, you are to ask him to fetch your mother. Thus the scene will be set for the theft.'

'Ah. I am beginning to see,' said Mrs Lessing. 'By presenting him with a valuable tiara lying on the ground you present him with an irresistible temptation—'

'And the perfect excuse if he is caught,' said Sophie triumphantly. 'If he is discovered with the tiara in his possession, he has only to claim that he was retrieving it for me, as it fell from my head when I swooned.'

'Exactly,' said Cicely. And he can do so safe in the knowledge that you will back him up. Once he has retrieved it, however, he will take it and sell it before fetching your mother. That way he can have the whole transaction—the theft and the sale—over with in a matter of fifteen minutes. After that, all he has to do then is find you, aunt, tell you Sophie is unwell, and take you to her. By the time anyone thinks to ask about the tiara he will have disappeared, so that he cannot be questioned.'

'And even if by some chance he is, he has only to claim he forgot all about it and never retrieved it, saying that some unscrupulous person must have made off with it whilst he was busy seeing to me,' said Sophie, seeing the beauty of the scheme.

'By which time the tiara will already have been dismantled,' said Cicely, 'with the jewels being sent off to various unsavoury jewellers who will sell them on for a huge profit—or so he will suppose.'

And there's the rub,' said Mrs Lessing. 'We might catch the thief, but the tiara will still be stolen.'

'That is where the private detectives come in,' said Alex. 'A couple of private detectives—already in Marienbad, at my request—will follow Goss from the Kurhaus, and apprehend him as he tries to sell the tiara.' He had been sitting quietly for the most part until now, allowing Cicely to explain, but here he took over. 'Goss's idea will be to sell the tiara at once. He will not be tempted to slip it into the pocket of an innocent passerby because the loss of the tiara will not be discovered for some time—Miss Lessing will be clearly too ill

215

to notice—and because, even if he is discovered in possession of it, he has only to say that he retrieved it when it slipped from her head and that he is intending to return it to her as soon as he has fetched her mother. And once in the jeweller's shop, there will be no innocent passers-by for him to incriminate.' He looked round at their interested faces. 'And that is when the detectives will strike.'

'Catching him in the very act of selling the stolen goods!' said Sophie, her eyes aglow with excitement.

'There will be no defence possible,' said Alex. 'He will be caught red-handed, and then he will be locked away for a very long time.'

'And the names of everyone who has ever been incriminated by him will be completely cleared,' said Cicely.

'An excellent plan,' declared Mrs Lessing roundly. 'Cicely, I have to hand it to you, my dear. It is a wonderful idea.'

Cicely's face fell a little. 'It is, as long as it works.'

She thought of Robert Burns's immortal phrase:

The best laid schemes o' mice an' men
Gang aft a-gley.

'You're thinking of Robbie Burns,' said Sophie, whose thoughts had followed her own. 'But it's still a good plan, even if it does go a-gley. And we shall just have to do our best to see that it doesn't.'

Their mood sobered. Despite Sophie's words, all four of them knew that things could easily go wrong.

However, it was worth a try.

'Now. To details,' said Mrs Lessing practically. 'When is this dinner party to take place?'

'A week on Friday.'

'A week on Friday?' asked Mrs Lessing, horrified. 'Cicely, it's impossible. I can't arrange a dinner party at such short notice.'

'I realize it's difficult,' said Cicely, 'but you know all the local dignitaries here, Aunt, and I am sure you can manage to arrange things. And as for the invitations, well, the season in Marienbad is so short that no one can give much warning of their festivities, so people are used to attending events at short notice.'

Mrs Lessing shook her head in disbelief. 'Even so, a week on Friday.'

'You can do it, Mother,' said Sophie, encouragingly.

Mrs Lessing looked doubtful. 'Well, I suppose I can try,' she said.

'I will be providing the tiara,' said Alex. 'I will bring it to the villa tomorrow, if I may.'

'You will be welcome at any time,' said Mrs Lessing graciously.

He inclined his head. 'Thank you.'

'And when does Martin Goss arrive?' asked

Sophie.

'On Monday,' said Cicely. 'Which means we have a few days to perfect our plan, and after that Al—Mr Evington and I must not be seen. Mr Evington will remain in Karlsbad, and I will remain at the villa. We don't want Goss to see us and scent a trap.'

'Very well.' Mrs Lessing finished her coffee and stood up.

Alex rose politely, and the two young ladies rose as well.

'We will expect you at the villa tomorrow, Mr Evington. I hope you will come to lunch. It will give us a chance to finalize the details of our plan.' By now, Mrs Lessing was as involved as the rest of them. 'And in the meantime, I have a lot of arranging to do.'

They made their farewells. Alex returned to the neighbouring town of Karlsbad and Cicely, together with her cousin and her aunt, returned to the villa.

*   *   *

Cicely felt uncomfortable as she walked through the pine forests surrounding her aunt's villa on the following morning. She had slept badly, her mind a whirl of dinners and tiaras, but most of all Alex . . . No matter how hard she tried, she could not put him out of her mind. She turned her attention to the forest, breathing in the heady scent of pine and rejoicing in the beauty of the trees. Beneath their needled branches the path was cool. Blue shadows fell across the undergrowth, pierced here and there by a brilliant shaft of sunlight that lanced into the forest's cool depths.

She began to feel her spirit calm. Her pace gradually slowed, until she was doing nothing more than strolling along the path. It would soon be over: Martin Goss would be caught; she would return to England; Alex would leave the Manor. And everything would be as it had been before.

But would it? Whilst a part of her hoped that would be the case, another part of her knew that, for her, nothing would ever be the same again.

She forced herself to turn her thoughts into less dangerous channels and began to take greater notice of her surroundings. She took in the ferns and brackens that grew beneath the trees, and stopped every now and again to let her eyes wander down over the glimpses of the spa town, which was just visible through their heavily needled branches.

By and by she began to feel better, and decided that, on reaching the next bend, she would turn back to the villa. It was already eleven o'clock, and she would have to change for luncheon at twelve.

She had almost reached the bend, and was preparing to turn, when she saw someone round it from the other direction. She stopped dead. It was Alex!

He too, stopped. By the look on his face it was obvious he was surprised to see her.

She took a deep breath to calm her pulse which had become uncomfortably rapid, and then managed to say a few words. 'I . . . was just taking a stroll before luncheon,' she began, suddenly feeling acutely aware of the fact that she had ventured out on her own and was now alone with him in the cool and inviting depths of the forest.

His eyes wandered over her face, as if taking in the softness of her hair and the delicate flush that had sprung to her cheek.

'I arrived early,' he said, by way of explanation. 'I didn't know how long it would take me to find the villa, and so I left in plenty of time. I didn't want to disturb your aunt before half-past twelve and so I decided to take a walk.'

They stood looking at each other, an indefinable awkwardness hanging between them. It should not have been there. Cicely was merely taking a stroll, and Alex was doing the same. They had simply met on the way. After expressing their surprise at seeing each other, they should have turned and walked back to the villa. Nothing would have been more natural. Instead of which they stood facing each other, neither one of them moving or speaking, as though in the grip of some invisible spell which held them rigid, afraid to move or speak for fear of losing control of what they might do or say.

'Cicely—'

'Alex—'

They spoke at last in an effort to break the tension that rippled through the forest air, but they spoke at the same time and it unnerved them, making them relapse into silence again. And it was just as well, for Cicely had the sudden feeling that if they succeeded in breaking the tension the storm would break with it; not a storm of thunder and lightning, but of feelings and passions that would be impossible to control.

There was only one thing to do. She must go back to the villa, and leave this highly charged atmosphere behind. She tried to turn around but it was beyond her power to do it. She made a determined attempt, and this time she managed.

It made things easier. She was no longer looking at Alex, and she began to walk away from him.

Until she heard his voice. 'I can't let you do it.'

She stopped. She knew she must keep on walking, but almost against her will she turned, and when she did so she caught her breath. There was an air of such intensity about him it seemed he was more alive than anything else in the forest. Against the suddenly dimmed background he stood out, his attitude one of tightly leashed power, as though he was a predator about to pounce. But it was not just his body that held her motionless, causing her heart to skip a beat. His face, a collection of sharp angles and planes, held her rigid, and his eyes burned.

She felt alarmed, not because of what he might do, but because of what they might do together. Yet despite this she was unable to move; unable to take the steps that would let her walk away.

Then she must say something. If she could not move she must at least utter a few words. The situation was becoming so charged with pent-up energy that she knew she must do something to give it release, for if it continued it would become unbearable. 'I . . . I don't know what . . .' She started to speak, but it was impossible for her to continue because her throat and mouth were parched.

His eyes continued to bore into her own, holding her and drinking her in.

She began to tingle.

And then he spoke. 'I can't let you marry Chuffington,' he said.

'Marry . . . ?' She couldn't think what he was talking about. Had she heard him correctly? There was such a rushing in her ears that she could not be sure. Her mind was no more help than her ears, for it was filled with heart-wrenching memories, and she was finding it

222

difficult to think. She was in the forest, with Alex, and his eyes were full of an intense emotion that she could not begin to understand; her legs were turning to water; but beyond that her mind could not go.

'It isn't worth it,' he said. His eyes still held her. 'I know life has been difficult for you, and I know he can give you a beautiful home, but—'

Cicely blinked. The rushing sound in her ears began to diminish.

He can give you a beautiful home?

'—you will not be happy,' he went on.

He can give you a beautiful home. The words began to sink in.

And her expression changed.

Gone was the rushing in her ears, and the weakness in her knees. In their place was a growing disdain. To begin with she had been perplexed that he should think she was going to marry Chuff Chuff, but realizing he thought she was going to marry him for Parmiston Manor her anger began to stir. Did he really know her so little? Did he hold her in such low esteem that he thought she would marry for reasons such as that?

'It isn't enough,' he said.

'Isn't it?' she demanded. She was by now almost back in control of herself.

He ignored her comment and walked towards her, his eyes fixed tumultuously on her own. She had never realized how deep they were before, as though they were whirlpools that could draw her in. She stood her ground as he approached her, but even so a part of her had an urge to back away. He was so overpoweringly, so overwhelmingly masculine. It was something she was able to forget on occasion, when it was hidden under a civilized veneer, but it was always there, waiting to break through. And it had broken through now, revealing the full strength and power of the man beneath.

'I can't let you do it,' he said again. He cupped her chin. 'You'll regret it.' He searched her eyes as though searching her soul. 'Chuffington's a buffoon—'

At his criticism of her childhood friend her anger began to rise again, and she used it to fight the unwanted sensations that were bubbling just beneath the surface, aroused by his touch. It would be so easy to let her eyes close; so easy to fall into his arms and turn up her face for his kiss, but she could not allow herself to do it. If she once surrendered to him she would do so completely; body, mind and soul. And she had no intention of surrendering herself to a man whose feelings were not clear to her. And so she focused on her anger, telling herself he had no right to speak of her childhood friend in that way.

'Lord Chuffington is a dear, sweet man,' she said, taking a step backwards and freeing herself from his touch. 'He has more virtues than you could possibly imagine. He—'

'Virtues!' He spoke contemptuously. 'You don't need virtues! You need a man who can show you what it is to be a woman. He can give you a safe life; an easy life; but there is more to life than ease and safety, Cicely.' His voice became husky. 'There is so much more.'

Looking at him standing before her she did not doubt it. Although she was a complete innocent in the ways of men and women, a part of her instinctively knew what he was talking about. It was as though his words had tapped into the primal heart of her, and she was filled with a sense of anticipation, as though something momentous was about to happen. His presence was so overpowering, the feelings he aroused in her so overwhelming, that she did not know how to control them. And if she lost control . . . but still she did not turn away. She was held there by his presence, and the searing energy flashing between them. She flexed her feet, but it did no good. She could not move. She was held fast by the overwhelming force that enveloped them, crackling all around them like a forest fire.

'There are kisses, for a start,' he said throatily. 'You have never been kissed, but—'

'Wrong,' she said breathlessly, remembering the gossamer-light brush of his lips against hers when they had been overtaken by their feelings once before. 'You kissed me—'

'In the study?' He shook his head. 'That wasn't a kiss.' He dragged her into his arms. '*This* is a kiss.'

His mouth closed over hers and the world disappeared. She was aware of nothing but Alex. It was as if there was no forest, no ground, no air and no sky; nothing but the searing heat of his body and his hot mouth claiming hers. Dominating, possessing, his tongue explored every inch of her mouth as her lips instinctively parted to let him in. His arms pressed her closer and then closer still as he crushed her body against him, until she could feel his every muscle, hard, firm and unyielding, pressed against her soft and pliant flesh.

Her hands rose of their own accord and slid round his neck. She was a willing partner in their mutual exploration, knowing on some deeply instinctive level that what they were doing was right. It felt so wonderful, opening up to her a whole new world, one she had never known existed. It was a world of heat and passion, of deep, intuitive feelings, of overwhelming sensations, and of pure unbridled joy. She had never known it was possible to feel like this, to be so close to another person, spiritually, physically and emotionally, that she felt she was melting into him. But she knew it now, and with every touch of his mouth, every brush of his hand, she was aware of it more and more.

She wanted it to go on for ever, and when his mouth left hers she gave an unwitting cry, feeling suddenly lost. But he had released her only so that he could pull back and look at her, drinking her in.

His dark eyes traced the delicate curves of her face, lingering on her cheeks, her eyelids, her chin and her brow, before they looked deeply into her own.

Then taking her face between his hands he caressed her, his strong thumbs following the line of her cheekbones until at last they held her face with a strength and delicacy that made her shiver to the depths of her soul. And then he kissed her again. Slowly, languorously, as if time did not matter, as if they had all eternity in which to discover each other.

His hands dropped to her shoulders and trailed a blaze of heat down her spine as they dropped lower, lower still . . .

In the background, she was dimly aware of a sound. Some small part of her, a part that had not yet completely succumbed to the intoxicating sensations that were coursing through her body, began to interpret it as church bells.

Alex released her slowly, reluctantly, as though it cost him an enormous effort, and yet he let her go. Gradually she began to emerge from her rapturous state and return to reality.

And reality was that the church bells were tolling the time, their ponderous chimes ringing out the hour of twelve. If she did not return at once to her aunt's villa she would be missed, for it was time to change for luncheon.

She stepped back, still dazed, and tried to collect herself. Steadying her rapid pulse, she smoothed her crumpled skirt and pinned her straying locks back in place. What had come over her? Why had she so forgotten herself that she had allowed him to kiss her, and even worse, responded?

The answer to that was all too clear. But it was not an answer she could allow herself to dwell on.

'I have to go,' she said.

She did not dare look at him. She was uncomfortably aware that his dark eyes were still full of desire and she knew that if she looked at him she would stay. Without waiting for him to reply she turned and ran down the forest path, not looking back. She arrived back at her aunt's villa ten minutes later flustered and out of breath. She slipped in at the door without ringing the bell and ran up to her room, not allowing herself to stop until she had closed the door behind her.

Fortunately, her aunt and cousin were in their rooms changing for luncheon, and had not noticed her absence. Even so, she must make sure she was composed before she appeared downstairs. She sat down on the edge of her bed and at last allowed herself to rest. Her breathing was coming thick and fast, and her feet were sore. She kicked off her shoes and luxuriated in the freedom it brought her: her shoes had been designed for gentle strolling on properly paved paths, not running over rough and uneven forest floors.

Why had Alex kissed her? she wondered as she began to regain her breath. Was it really nothing more then a desire for dalliance? She did not think so. His kiss had been too intense. It had carried the full weight of his heart and soul behind it. Or at least, so it had seemed to her. But she had to admit that she was inexperienced in such matters. Oh, it was so perplexing! For all she knew, it could have been motivated solely by a desire to stop her marrying Lord Chuffington. But that would imply jealousy, and why would he be jealous if he did not have any feelings for her?

This thought was too difficult to answer, and so she turned her attention to the problem of why he had told her that she couldn't marry Lord Chuffington in the first place. What had given him the preposterous idea she was likely to do so?

She would have told him that he was mistaken if he had given her a chance, but just as she had been about to do so he had accused her of being about to marry for position and a manor house, and then, before she could gather her scattered wits, he had driven all thought of anything else out of her mind by kissing her.

That wasn't a kiss. This is a kiss.

His words came back to her. Oh, yes, that *was* a kiss. It had been like nothing she had ever experienced before, and deep in the heart of her she knew that she wanted to experience it again. But she could not allow herself to do so. No matter how right it had felt, she had no clear idea of Alex's feelings for her, and without such knowledge she could not let him kiss her again. Had his kiss been born of genuine feeling? she wondered, or had it been born of a simple desire to stop her marrying Chuffington?

She shook her head. It was such a puzzle. His feelings were as mysterious to her now as they had ever been. She had, however, a clear idea of her feelings for him, and they were deep and all-encompassing. The respect she felt for the way he had risen from poverty was matched by her enjoyment of his personality, which gave her a deep and abiding pleasure in his company. For the first time in her life she had met a man with whom she could share joint ventures. She thought of the way they had worked so well together when dealing with the business of the Manor, and how they had helped each other to make plans for catching a thief. Alex was a man she could esteem and trust. And the effect he had on her whenever he was near her deepened those feelings, transforming them into something altogether more magical. Love.

She had always wondered how love would feel. Now she knew. It felt wonderful.

Or would do, if her love was returned.

Which brought her full circle. What did Alex feel for her?

Attempting to put the unanswerable question out of her mind she began to change, taking off her plain skirt and blouse and changing them for something more modish. As she did so she could not help wishing that the present customs did not demand her to change her clothes several times a day. One outfit for the daytime and another for evening seemed to her to be quite sufficient. Still, she could not run contrary to society in every way, and so she donned a simple day dress in a tiny blue-and-white check, with a high neckline, sashed waist and long sleeves, before going downstairs for luncheon.

She had by now completely recovered from her exertions, and bore no visible traces of what had just happened.

'Ah! Just in time,' said her aunt, as she went into the sitting-room. 'It is half past twelve. Mr Evington should be here any minute, and then we will go into lunch.'

Making no mention of the fact that she had already seen Mr Evington that morning, Cicely set about composing herself, knowing that she must be able to spend the next few hours in his company without becoming distracted by wayward thoughts.

True to her aunt's prediction, Alex was at that moment announced. He greeted Sophie and Mrs Lessing then turned to Cicely politely, giving no sign that anything untoward had passed between them. For this Cicely was grateful. The luncheon was going to be difficult enough for her as it was—a smouldering glance would have made it impossible.

Fortunately, Mrs Lessing, as hostess, did most of the talking for the next ten minutes. She made Mr Evington feel at home, then arranged everything as they went through into the dining-room for lunch.

Once the first course—a clear soup—had been served, the conversation turned to the matter of the theft.

'I have managed to take the Kurhaus,' said Mrs Lessing, as they began to eat. 'I have had to pull any number of strings, and call in one or two favours as well, but it is done. Unfortunately, however, I have not been able to take it for Friday.'

Cicely looked up. This was an unwelcome complication.

'We will have to amend our plans slightly, that is all,' said Mrs Lessing, 'and stage the theft for Wednesday.'

'That doesn't give us much time,' said Cicely, not liking the change in the arrangement. 'Martin Goss won't arrive in Marienbad until Monday. You then have to arrange to make his acquaintance and invite him to the dinner. I don't see how it can be done in such a short space of time.'

'I've thought of a way round that,' said Sophie exuberantly. 'We don't need to make his acquaintance at all—at least not properly, by waiting for someone to introduce us. There is another way.'

'Not a way I like,' put in her mother reprovingly.

'But it will work.' Sophie turned to Cicely. 'I mean to bump into him on the promenade, which will cut out all need for a formal introduction. "So silly of me", I will say, fluttering my eyelashes. "I cannot have been looking where I was going". He will say, "It is quite all right, Miss . . . ?" I will introduce myself, he will doff his hat and introduce himself—to Mother, of course, observing the niceties—and then, apparently wanting to make up for bumping into him I will tell him he must let me make amends by inviting him to our dinner party.'

'It's a good idea,' said Alex approvingly. 'Goss is a vain man. He will be flattered by your attention, and he is therefore likely to accept the invitation. Engaging in a flirtation with a pretty young woman is just his style.'

'I think it's a dreadful idea,' declared Mrs Lessing, putting down her spoon with a determined clatter. 'You were not brought up to play the coquette,' she said to Sophie. 'You were brought up to be well behaved.'

'But Mother, it is only acting,' said Sophie appealingly.

Mrs Lessing shook her head. 'I would rather we could think of another way.'

'But that's just it,' said Sophie with a sigh. 'We can't.'

'And we do have to make sure Goss attends the dinner party,' Cicely reminded her aunt.

'I suppose so,' said Mrs Lessing with a frown.

'And it is in a good cause,' Sophie reminded her.

'I wish there was another way,' said Mrs Lessing again, 'but if there isn't then we must go ahead with it. I just hope, after all this, we catch the wretched man, that's all.' She turned to Sophie. 'And you, miss, will see that no one we know is close by when you do your bumping trick.' Having voiced her concerns, Mrs Lessing became practical again. 'Now, as to who else is to be invited to the party . . .'

Mrs Lessing outlined her plans for the dinner party, ending by saying, 'I have made out the guest list, but I will need help with the invitations.'

'Sophie and I will help you write them this afternoon,' said Cicely.

'Meanwhile, I will give the private detectives their instructions, and make sure they know exactly what they are to do,' said Alex. 'As to the tiara . . .' He pulled a box out of the inside pocket of his jacket and laid it on the table. He lifted the lid. Inside was an exquisite tiara. It was made of diamonds, with three sapphires set into the rim.

Sophie gasped.

'That will certainly tempt him,' said Mrs Lessing. She frowned. 'Sophie will not be in any danger, will she? He is not likely to harm her in any way? Because if he is, then this ends now.'

'No.' Alex spoke certainly. 'Goss has never been guilty of violence. Stealth is his style. Sophie will not be in any danger.'

'Even so.' Cicely spoke out boldly. She had a feeling that Alex would not like what she was about to say, but her mind was made up. 'I intend to be outside the Kurhaus in case anything goes wrong.'

'That's impossible—' began Alex.

Cicely cut across him. 'I know what you are going to say, that he will recognize me, but I have thought it all out. I will be dressed in some of my aunt's old mourning clothes—that is, if you will lend them to me, Aunt?—and will be swathed from head to foot in black, making me appear older than my years. In addition, I will be wearing a large hat complete with veil, so that my face will be hidden. There is no way that Goss will recognize me in such an outfit, even if he sees me. And I mean to make sure that he doesn't see me. I will keep well hidden—something the dull black material of

235

the mourning clothes will make easy as it is specially designed to soak up the light. Without any hint of a glint or sparkle I will blend in with the shadows and be virtually invisible. But I will be on hand if Sophie needs any help.'

And if I forbid it?' asked Alex, his eyes fixed on her own.

She turned towards him innocently.

He gave a wry smile. 'You will do it anyway.' Then he became serious. 'In that case, I intend to be there as well. Like you, I will keep well hidden, and will wear concealing clothes, so that even if Goss spots me he will not recognize me.'

Sophie breathed a sigh of relief. 'Good. I didn't want you to think I was nervous, but I will feel better if you are nearby.'

'Then it is all settled.' Alex rose. 'Now I must be going. Thank you for a delightful luncheon,' he said to Mrs Lessing. And then, to all three ladies, 'I think it better if, until the night of the dinner party, we do not see each other again.'

His eyes drifted to Cicely as he said it.

Was that regret she saw there? she wondered. Or had she simply imagined it?

CHAPTER NINE

Cicely, Sophie and Mrs Lessing rose early the next morning: the two girls felt in need of a visit to the Kurhaus in order to rehearse their plan. Sophie wanted to work out the route she would take with Martin Goss and decide at which point she would swoon, Cicely wanted to find a good spot from which to keep an eye on the proceedings, whilst Mrs Lessing, declaring they could not go unchaperoned, accompanied them.

The morning was fine. Cicely had been blessed with good weather throughout her stay, for sunshine was in no way guaranteed in the spa town. The climate at Marienbad was similar to England's, it was often cool in the summer and it frequently rained.

The stroll to the Kurhaus was delightful. The band was playing and there was a holiday atmosphere, with many of the great and the good enjoying a brief respite from the pressures of their everyday lives. The English maintained a strong presence in the town, drawn by the magnet of their king. There was the prime minister and a number of other politicians, as well as Sir Herbert Beerbohm-Tree, the great actor and owner of His Majesty's Theatre in London. Then, too, there were a great many English ladies, all discreetly dressed in elegant coats and skirts, sharply contrasting with the Continental ladies, whose lace and frills seemed, to Cicely's mind, out of place in the early morning, being more suited to evening wear. Still, they added to the cosmopolitan air of the place, and provided an interesting change from being at home.

Once outside the Kurhaus Sophie paced out several routes before settling on one that would lead her in the direction of a convenient bench. 'If I swoon here,' she said, indicating the spot with her parasol, 'then Mr Goss can help me to the bench before going to fetch my mother.'

'Yes,' said Cicely. 'It seems to be a good place. How are you coming on with your swoon? Have you been able to make your tiara fall off?'

'Not yet,' Sophie admitted. 'The difficult part is deciding how firmly to attach it to my head. Too firmly, and it won't fall off; not firmly enough, and it falls off too soon. But I will practise again when we get home. Don't forget that, if the worst comes to the worst, I can always pass a hand over my brow and knock it off.'

'As long as it looks natural,' said Cicely. 'The important thing is to make sure it ends up on the ground. It doesn't really matter how it becomes dislodged.' She glanced at the spot again thoughtfully, and then glanced at the bench. Looking up, she cast her eyes around for a suitable place in which to hide.

'How about the doorway over there?' suggested Sophie.

Cicely's eyes followed the direction of Sophie's hand. Across from the spot where Sophie intended to swoon there was a convenient doorway, just around a corner, which was suitably inconspicuous, but at the same time it was near enough for her to be able to witness the scene. With luck, it should be a good place from which to watch the proceedings. Still, it was best to make sure.

'Wait here,' Cicely said. 'When I get to the corner and take up my position, I want to know whether you can see me.'

She strolled over to the corner and stepped into the doorway, then turned. From her viewpoint she could see both the bench and the spot where Sophie intended to swoon. Yes, it was the very spot. Just one more thing to check.

'Could you see me?' she asked, as she went back to Sophie.

'Not when you drew back,' said Sophie. As long as you don't stand too far forward you should not be noticed; particularly as it will be dark, and Martin Goss will not be looking for you.'

'Very well. It's settled. I suggest we go for a coffee now, in one of the cafés, and then go back to the villa so that you can practise your swooning again.'

Sophie agreed. 'I won't rest until I can dislodge the tiara every time.'

*   *   *

'He's here.' Mrs Lessing's voice held a note of satisfaction the following morning as she returned from a visit to her friend, Mrs Lincoln, who lived close by. 'I asked Mrs Lincoln casually if there were any new visitors to town today—it is a source of great interest to us in the summertime, and we always ask each other who has arrived, so the question did not seem unusual—and the Honourable Martin Goss was one of the names she mentioned.'

Cicely spoke calmly. 'Then it is time to put the first part of our plan into operation.'

She suppressed a feeling of being left out as Sophie and Mrs Lessing put on their outdoor things and prepared to leave for a walk on the promenade. She consoled herself with the fact that she would be able to watch the proceedings on the night of the dinner party, and helped Sophie to arrange her hat.

'You remember what he looks like?' asked Cicely, wanting to make sure her aunt and cousin would recognize him.

Mrs Lessing nodded. Cicely had given her a full description of the man.

'Good,' said Cicely.

'Wish me luck!' said Sophie, as she stuck the

240

hatpin into her hair. Her eyes were shining at the thought of the excitement to come.

'You might not see him today, remember,' Cicely cautioned her. 'He might be tired, and spend the rest of the day in his hotel.'

'Then we will have to try again tomorrow,' said Sophie. But the sooner we meet him the better. That way, there is more chance of him accepting our invitation.'

Cicely waved her aunt and cousin goodbye, and then sat down with a book. But for once Mr Wodehouse's glorious comic characters could not hold her interest. She set aside *The Pothunters* and strolled over to the window. Somewhere down in Marienbad, her aunt and cousin were seeking to draw Martin Goss into their trap. Cicely, however, must not be seen, which meant that her movements over the next few days would be necessarily restricted. However, she was too restless to remain in the villa, and putting on her coat she went out into the wonderfully scented pine forest that surrounded it.

She could not help her thoughts drifting back to her encounter with Alex as she walked through the trees, no matter how hard she had tried to put it out of her mind. She wished she understood him. Why had he objected to her marrying Chuff Chuff? What, indeed, had put the idea into his head? And why had he kissed her, driving all thought of everything else out of her mind?

She recalled the daydreams of her childhood, when she had imagined herself playing on the lawns of the Manor with her children, as Haringays had done for time out of mind. But in those daydreams the face of her husband had been vague. Now it was clear. It was the face of Alex Evington.

How strange it was, to find herself in love with Alex Evington. She had been so determined to dislike him. But it had become impossible for her to do anything but love him. He was everything she admired and valued, and yet for all his perplexing behaviour in kissing her she knew she must hide her feelings, for he had made it quite clear that he intended to sell the Manor as soon as he had caught Martin Goss, and then return to London. That being so, she knew that his feelings for her were not of a serious kind. He might kiss her in the madness of the moment, but he had no ideas beyond that or he would not be intending to quit the Manor, and she must school herself to forget him.

Something she was beginning to fear would be impossible.

Nevertheless, she was determined to try.

At last she returned to the villa, having rid herself of her restlessness by her walk, and found that Sophie and Mrs Lessing had just returned.

Sophie was in a state of great excitement.

'We've managed it!' she said as she took off

her coat. 'The Honourable Martin Goss is coming to the dinner party at the Kurhaus? He accepted our invitation!'

'It couldn't have been more fortunate,' said Mrs Lessing. 'As soon as I saw him I recognized him from your description, but his identity was confirmed by an elderly dowager walking past at that moment and returning his greeting by nodding, and saying shortly, "Goss".'

'So we were then absolutely certain it was him,' said Sophie, as the three of them went into the sitting-room. 'Oh, Cicely, I wish you could have been there! It all went according to plan. I bumped into him, flushed prettily—'

'Really, Sophie,' scolded her mother, 'I don't like to hear you describing yourself as pretty. It is unbecoming for a young lady to flatter herself.'

'Well, I did,' said Sophie unrepentantly, 'for there would have been no point in flushing unattractively.' Then, turning back to Cicely, she said, 'I fluttered my eyelashes and simpered and flirted, and through it all I squeezed out an incoherent apology. He raised his hat and smiled indulgently, and said, "No harm done", and I said he must let me make amends. And then I invited him to dinner. He looked as though he was going to refuse—my heart was in my mouth!—but then he caught sight of Mother. He could see she didn't half like the idea, for she couldn't disguise her true

243

feelings however much she tried, and as soon as she bridled I knew he would come. Annoying people is one of his greatest pleasures!'

'Really, Sophie, you don't know that,' reproved her mother.

'Well, by the look on his face it seemed that way,' said Sophie. And then he said, "If you are sure I would be welcome", in just such a way that Mother couldn't possibly refuse, so she issued him a stiff invitation.'

'And he accepted?' asked Cicely.

'He did—although as much to spite Mother as to spend the evening with me, I am sure!'

Cicely smiled. She could just imagine Martin Goss enjoying the situation, and exploiting it to the full.

'So he is coming!' said Sophie. 'Now all we have to do is make sure he steals the tiara and we have him.'

'One plan has already failed,' Cicely reminded her, not wanting her to get her hopes up too much.

'True,' said Sophie. Then added mischievously, 'But you didn't have me to help you then!'

Cicely laughed.

Mrs Lessing, however, was not amused, wondering aloud how her daughter had grown into such a minx.

Nevertheless, it was a buoyant party who sat down to tea. The first part of the venture had succeeded. Now they must hope for similar success in the second.

*　　　*　　　*

Cicely regarded herself in the glass. Swathed in an old black mourning dress of her aunt's, she gave the impression of being an elderly dowager instead of a young lady. Her ash-blonde hair was hidden by a wide-brimmed black hat and her face was covered with a thick veil. All in all, she was pleased with her disguise. Not only did it make her appear to be much older, it would also allow her to blend into the shadows. The heavy black fabric soaked up the light, as did the lace of the veil. Now all she needed to do was put on her coat when the time came for her to leave the villa and she would be ready to go.

She glanced at the clock. It was only half past nine. It was still too soon for her to set out.

It had been agreed that Sophie would swoon at half-past ten, and Cicely meant to be in place just before then. From her vantage point in the doorway she would be able to see everything that happened, and go to Sophie's aid if the situation should turn unexpectedly ugly. Alex, too, would be there, hidden across the road from Cicely, ready to lend his assistance if it should be required. But if all went well neither he nor Cicely would need to take a hand. Martin Goss would take the tiara and head for the shop, where the two private detectives would apprehend him in the act of trying to sell it.

Cicely went over to the window and looked out at the night. To her relief it was fine and clear. Rain would have spoilt their plan completely—Sophie could hardly have suggested a walk if it had been pouring down! But fortune had favoured them, and soon she would be on her way.

She tried to read, but she could not keep her attention on the novel, no matter how entertaining, because she was engaged in a far more entertaining enterprise of her own.

At last it was time to go. Slipping into one of her aunt's coats she lowered her veil then left the villa, setting out on foot for the Kurhaus.

Half an hour later, she was safely ensconced in the doorway, waiting for Sophie to appear.

The time passed slowly. She was cramped in the confines of the doorway but dare not leave it in case Sophie and Martin Goss, coming out of the Kurhaus, should see her. She stamped her feet and blew into her hands to ward off the cold.

Five minutes passed, then ten, and Cicely began to grow anxious. Sophie should have made an appearance by now. Try as she might, Cicely could not prevent herself from imagining the various things that could have gone wrong. Martin Goss might have failed to appear at the dinner party; he might have been impervious to Sophie's charms; or he might have seen a piece of jewellery that was more to his liking and decided to ignore the tiara.

The latter was a problem Cicely had always known they would face. Her aunt's guests were wealthy people, and the ladies would inevitably be wearing their jewels. If Goss saw something he felt would make a better target for his light fingers—

But wait. What was that? The sound of a woman's voice? It was Sophie's laughter, borne to her on the wind.

Hastily she pressed herself back into the doorway. By angling herself in exactly the right position she was able to see what was happening without being seen.

Yes. Sophie had managed to get Martin Goss to escort her outside. The two of them were approaching the place where Sophie had arranged to swoon. Sophie was looking beautiful in an off-the-shoulder evening gown, and it was no surprise that Martin Goss, resplendent in evening dress, should have been delighted with the idea of escorting her outside, even had she not been wearing a magnificent tiara. But the tiara was there, glinting in the moon-and-starlight. Cicely held her breath. They had reached the spot where Sophie intended to swoon—and now Sophie was swooning, and the tiara, just as they had practised it, was slipping from her head. Their plan was working.

Even so, Cicely hardly dared to breathe as Martin Goss helped Sophie to the bench, where she gracefully sank down in an attitude of complete helplessness. Martin Goss evidently said a few words to her—he is promising to fetch her mother, thought Cicely with satisfaction—and then Sophie fell back again in a most convincing fashion, whilst Goss left her side.

Cicely watched him head back towards the Kurhaus. Cicely was on tenterhooks. Would he take the tiara? She hardly dare look as she saw him approach it. He stopped, looked back to make sure that Sophie was indeed unconscious—or at least appeared to be so— then, with a furtive look round, he bent and picked up the tiara, which he slipped into his pocket.

Cicely let out her breath. So far so good.

She continued to watch as he hurried on, past the Kurhaus and up the street that led to the shop. She felt a surge of jubilation rising inside her. They had done it!

A minute later she sobered. There were still a number of things that could go wrong. Martin Goss might have a different contact in Marienbad, one they knew nothing about. Or he might decide to go to Karlsbad, or another of the neighbouring towns, to get rid of the tiara.

But it wasn't likely.

Sophie, still in character, was draped beautifully across the bench in case Goss should return. Cicely could not help admiring her style. Lillie Langtry, who had been the darling of Edward VII before she had become a notable actress, could not have done it better!

Still, the next fifteen minutes were tense. Cicely longed to leave the doorway and stretch her legs, but she dared not move. If anything went wrong and Goss returned she did not want to rouse his suspicions. So she must wait until Alex, who was to discreetly follow Goss, returned to tell her that it had all gone according to plan.

The minutes ticked by. She saw Sophie stir once or twice before sitting up, though in a pose which still suggested a recent swoon. If all went well, Goss would not return. But until they were sure he had been apprehended Sophie must continue to play her part.

The church clock chimed eleven. Surely it would not be much longer?

But no! There was Alex, hurrying towards her along the empty street.

'We've got him!' he exclaimed as he joined her in the doorway.

'At last!' Cicely was delighted.

She lifted her veil, which was beginning to stifle her, and threw it back over her hat. It caught on the pin. She raised her hands to free it, only to find them brushing Alex's strong fingers, as he too moved to release her veil. She stilled, her mouth a round 'o' as she looked up into his face. His expression was penetrating. He was looking down at her with the light of passion burning in his eyes. She felt his fingers close round her hands. Then he drew them to his lips. A tingling sensation spread over her skin, despite her gloves: the electricity that coursed through her whenever he touched her could not be stopped by mere lace. He turned her hands over and kissed her palms. She shuddered, the power of his touch sending waves of desire through her.

'Well? Did we get him?'

Sophie's voice broke into their private moment, and Cicely quickly withdrew her hands, so that by the time Sophie reached them there was nothing untoward for her to see. Fortunately, Alex's back had blocked her view of what had just happened, for innocent though the gesture had been in one way, in another it had been full of forbidden passion.

Alex's features were instantly back under control. It called forth Cicely's admiration—before making her wonder if it was indicative, not so much of control, but of a lack of serious intention. If his kiss had been the instinct of a moment, the attraction of a man for a woman, then arranging his features would not have cost him any effort at all. She realized it with a deflated feeling. Still, she must not let it show.

'Yes.' Alex replied to Sophie's question. 'He

went to the man we hoped he would use, and was in the process of negotiating a price for the tiara when the two private detectives I'd hired took him in charge.'

'Do we have him? Really have him?' asked Cicely. 'Will the police be able to make the charges stick?'

Alex nodded. 'They will have sworn statements from us saying what took place here tonight—leaving out the part about it being a trap, of course—and the testimony of the private detectives. The Honourable Martin Goss will be going away for a very long time.'

'Hooray!' said Sophie. 'Then I had better be getting back to the dinner party. It will be finishing soon. All of Mother's guests are at the spa for the good of their health, and the evening will end at an early hour. Wait for us in an inconspicuous corner of the Kurhaus. I know Mother wants to invite you back to the villa for coffee,' she said to Alex. 'She wants to hear all about it.'

Cicely and Alex escorted Sophie back to the Kurhaus, where the dinner party was already breaking up. They stayed in the background whilst Sophie and her mother said goodbye to all their guests, and then the four of them returned to the villa, where they set about talking over the night's events over a cup of coffee.

'I am so relieved it all went well,' said Mrs Lessing, who had not liked the scheme and

251

had doubted the wisdom of going along with it, despite her agreement. She had been particularly anxious when Sophie had walked out of the Kurhaus with Martin Goss, and had almost called a halt to the proceedings there and then. Even the knowledge that Alex and Cicely would be keeping an eye on Sophie had not completely stilled her maternal worries. But still, it was over now, and successfully so. Martin Goss had been caught.

'Your sister will at last be vindicated,' said Sophie, who had heard all about Katie's ordeal at the hands of Martin Goss.

'Yes.' A look of satisfaction crossed his face. 'She is no longer in service, so in one way it no longer matters, but she will still be delighted to know that no one will now believe she stole that wretched bracelet.'

'And Gladys, too, will be vindicated,' said Cicely. 'I will make sure that news of Goss's arrest reaches everyone who attended the ball at Oakleigh Manor, so that no one will be left with any suspicions about her honesty.'

'A very satisfying evening,' said Mrs Lessing, relaxing now that it had come to a close.

The servants came in to remove the tray and Alex rose.

'Very satisfying,' he agreed. 'But now, it's late. I must be getting back to Karlsbad.'

'Must you go so soon?' asked Sophie.

He gave her a tolerant smile. 'It is almost two o'clock. Good night,' he said to Mrs

Lessing. He turned to Cicely. His eyes lingered on hers. 'Good night,' he said softly.

'Good night,' she returned.

And then he was gone.

*   *   *

Alone in her room some half an hour later, Cicely began to tidy away her things. She had dropped her aunt's black coat and hat on the bed when she had returned from the Kurhaus and, as the servants had not been into her room since then, she had to clear them away before she could settle down to sleep. She arranged her aunt's coat over the back of the chair that stood in front of the dressing-table and then picked up the matching hat. It was when she had thrown back the veil, she thought as she straightened the lace, that Alex had reached up to help her. She could still remember the way it had felt when his hands had closed around hers. The memory of it was so strong that she could almost feel the touch of his fingers even now.

But it would not be wise to encourage such feelings. She must put the hat away. In fact, she would put it away in the wardrobe until the morning, she thought resolutely, for if she left it on the dressing-table she feared it would colour her dreams.

She crossed the room to the wardrobe—and stopped suddenly, her heart pounding in her chest. For there, in the corner, almost hidden by the shadows next to the wardrobe, was a dark figure, unfolding itself from its hiding place. She stood still, frozen, and then backed away, even as her eyes widened in fear. Pushing himself out of the shadows was . . . Martin Goss.

'No,' she gasped. 'It can't be.'

'Can't be what?' he asked menacingly, stepping forward into the candlelight.

His appearance was immaculate. His double-breasted jacket with its long tails, wing-collared shirt, tailored trousers and flat pumps, were the hallmark of a civilized gentleman. But his blue eyes held an evil gleam.

Cicely's eyes dropped to his hands. He was holding something between them. It was the sash from one of her evening dresses. As she watched, he stretched it between his hands, wrapping one end round each hand in a menacing manner before snapping it in the most alarming way.

There was no doubting his purpose. He meant to strangle her. But how had he known she was involved? And how had he known where to find her? And how had he escaped from the detectives? She wanted to know the answers to those questions, but even more she wanted to make him talk to her so that she would have time to try and think of a way out of the terrible situation.

'How did you find me?' she asked.

He gave a crooked smile. 'Find you? I didn't find you—that was just a lucky chance. I found—or wanted to find—Miss Lessing.' His voice became hard. 'Because the charming Miss Lessing set a trap for me.'

'How . . .?' Cicely's voice was quavering. 'How did you know?' she asked, wondering where their plan had gone wrong.

'As soon as the detectives revealed themselves I knew I'd been had, and it didn't take me long to work out who'd had me. The oh-so-charming Miss Lessing, who just happened to bump into me on the promenade and just happened to invite me to her mother's dinner party, before inducing me to take her outside, where she conveniently lost her tiara whilst appearing to swoon. It was a good plan. It's just a pity—for you—the detectives weren't up to the job. They thought they'd got me, but once out of the shop I gave them the slip. And then I wanted revenge.'

'But how did you find the villa?' demanded Cicely. 'You had no way of knowing where Miss Lessing lived.'

'Hadn't I, though? I had already made it my business to find out—although I must admit, it was originally for different purposes. I'm in low water, and Miss Lessing is a pretty young heiress; moreover, a pretty young heiress who'd taken a fancy to me—or at least, that's how it seemed when she bumped into me on the promenade. I thought she was the answer to my prayers. So as soon as I'd accepted her invitation to the dinner party I made it my business to discover where she lived. In fact, I found out all about her. Where she went, what she did, what she liked and disliked, and—oh, yes—what kind of dowry she was likely to have.'

'So you intended to marry her,' said Cicely, realizing that this was why Goss had made so many enquiries.

'I did.' His eyes hardened. 'Until she played me for a fool, and nearly put me in prison. Whereupon I intended to exact my revenge. I sneaked into the house—not difficult, as you were all out and only a handful of old servants were left behind—and found the young lady's room, intending to pay her back for what she had tried to do to me. It wasn't hard to tell which one was hers. It had a lot of pretty clothes in the wardrobe, the sort a young lady would wear—only at the time I didn't realize there were two young ladies in the house. Until you walked into the room. And then, in a blinding flash, I saw the whole thing. That you were behind it, and Miss Lessing was just doing what she was told. I should have seen it coming. Miss Lessing had no reason to trap me. She didn't even know me. But you did. You were there at the Manor, and you knew who was really behind the theft of the necklace. So you decided to set a trap.'

'You deserved it,' said Cicely recklessly.

'You caused an innocent young girl to be accused of your crime.'

He made a derogatory exclamation. 'Innocent young girl? She was a maid. What did it matter? You of all people should know that servants don't count.'

'They count every bit as much as you and me,' said Cicely hotly, realizing that Alex had had some reason to take against the landed classes. Goss was everything that was corrupt and disgraceful.

He sneered. 'Every bit as much as you, perhaps,' he said, flexing the scarf between his hands again. 'But no one matters as much as me.'

He took a step towards her and Cicely shrank back. She was under no illusions as to what he intended to do with the scarf. Her hand went instinctively to her neck.

'Don't worry,' he said evilly. 'It won't hurt— much.'

He lunged towards her and she held up the hat, which was still grasped between her fingers, in a useless gesture of defence . . . and then saw the candlelight gleam on the head of the hat pin. She was saved! If only she could pull it out in time . . .

He closed the distance between them, throwing the scarf round her neck and pulling it tight. She fought down an impulse to raise her hands to her throat and instead focused all her energies on drawing the wicked long pin out of the hat. It flashed momentarily in the candlelight as she pulled it free, and then she brought it down with all the strength she could muster, driving it into his hand.

He let out an exclamation of pain and she felt the pressure go from her neck as he dropped the scarf and clutched his injured hand, which was dripping with blood.

'You bitch!' he shouted.

Eyes watering, coughing and wheezing as she gasped in lungfuls of air, Cicely nevertheless braced herself for a renewed attack. She held the hat pin aloft, ready to defend herself.

Martin looked at the wicked pin and then at Cicely's determined face. His eyes went beyond her, over her shoulder to the door.

For one moment, Cicely was tempted to step out of the way. If his route to the door was clear she felt he would make his escape. She nearly moved aside. But then she remembered that Sophie and Mrs Lessing were in the villa. If Goss should come upon them, there was no telling what he would do. She raised the pin still higher and stood her ground.

'You bloody little bitch!' he spat. Then, darting suddenly over to the window he threw it open and climbed out.

Cicely willed herself to follow him but she felt dizzy and weak, and knew she would never be able to climb out of the window in her present condition. She was still not breathing properly, her throat being bruised and sore, and without proper lungfuls of air she could do no more than collapse on to the bed.

Still, at least he had been foiled. He had not managed to harm her. Nor would he be able to harm Sophie or her aunt. She must content herself with that thought, she realized, as the pin dropped out of her nerveless fingers and fell to the floor.

*　　　*　　　*

Outside in the drive, Alex was finishing his cigar. He had not smoked inside as he knew Mrs Lessing did not like it, but he had lit a cigar on leaving the villa. He was drawing it out, smoking it as slowly as possible, because he was loth to go. He did not want to leave Cicely. He wanted to stride back into the villa, take the stairs three at a time to her room, throw open her door and demand that she give up the idea of marrying Lord Chuffington.

His cigar finished, he threw the butt down on to the drive and ground it beneath his foot, as he wanted to grind anyone who threatened to take Cicely away from him . . .

The strength of his feelings took him by surprise. He had never felt so strongly about anyone before, but Cicely provoked in him all manner of new emotions. She was the most surprising, perplexing yet adorable woman he had ever met, and she drove him to distraction.

If only he could go back into the villa . . . but he knew he could not. Still, even though his cigar was now finished, he could not bring himself to leave. He walked round to the side of the villa, looking up at the windows.

He was behaving like a lovesick boy, he thought uncomfortably. And yet he could not help himself.

He wondered which room was hers.

A moment later he had his answer, as he could see her graceful figure silhouetted against the blind at the last window. Her hand was raised. She must be about to unpin her hair. How long was it? he wondered. Strands of her hair had come loose on several occasions, and he had revelled in the sensuous feel of them beneath his hand as he had pushed them back into place, but he did not know exactly how long her tresses were. Would they fall to her shoulders when her hair was unpinned? he wondered longingly. Halfway down her back? Or to her waist?

But no. She was not unpinning her hair, he realized with a frown. What, then, was she doing? She was standing in a most unnatural attitude, leaning backwards as though she was in fear of being attacked. He was immediately alert. Something was wrong. His instinct was confirmed a moment later when he saw a second figure outlined at the window, the figure of a man.

He began to run towards the window, covering the ground with long strides. Then the window was thrown open and the man, whoever he was, illumined by the candlelight from within the room, climbed out.

Alex froze for a second as he recognized the gleaming blond hair of Martin Goss.

Goss? Here? But how?

There was no time for further thought. In one fluid movement he moved to intercept him, tackling him as he dropped to the ground. There was a scuffle, and then Alex ended it with a well-placed blow.

As he did so, the two detectives came running up.

'What in hell's name is going on?' demanded Alex, furiously, as he handed Goss over to them.

'He gave us the slip,' said the first man, shifting his feet, whilst the second one looked sheepish.

'Your excuses will have to wait. I haven't got time for this now,' he said, knowing Cicely was in the villa, possibly frightened or hurt. 'Later,' he said commandingly before rushing into the villa.

Pushing aside the startled butler who opened the door, he was about to climb the stairs to Cicely's room when he saw her coming down. She was white and shaken but appeared to be unhurt.

'Are you all right?' he demanded. His body flooded with relief at the sight of her, for he had feared the worst.

'Goss.' The word came out as a hoarse whisper.

'It's all right. He won't bother you any more. He's outside now, in the charge of the detectives. They won't let him escape again.' He was about to go on, but she had by now reached the bottom of the stairs and he could see by the glare of the gaslight that she was far from well. 'What is it?' he asked in concern. Then he saw the bruises which were beginning to rise round her neck and throat, showing up darkly against the high neck of her dress. 'In here.' He lifted her from her feet, one arm under her knees and the other one round her shoulders, and carried her into the drawing-room, where he set her down gently on the sofa.

She lay back, relieved that she could give in to her weakness now that Alex was there. She had struggled against it, but she had to admit defeat. Her throat and neck were sore, and she wanted nothing more than to rest until she should have regained her strength.

'What happened?' he asked in concern.

'Goss—' The word, again, was no more than a hoarse whisper.

'Don't speak,' he said. 'I can guess. From the look of it he tried to strangle you.'

He felt his rage rising as he said it. It was a

good thing that Goss was not there, but was safely in the custody of the detectives, otherwise he would not have been responsible for his actions.

Gently he began to undo the top few buttons of her dress, which had a high neck reaching to her ears. As he pushed the black fabric aside he saw the full extent of her injuries. Then heard an outraged cry from the doorway.

'Take your hands from my niece.'

He looked up to see Mrs Lessing framed in the doorway.

'I thought better of you,' she said, eyes flaring. 'I thought you were a gentleman.'

'Cicely's been attacked,' he said shortly. 'Goss gave the detectives the slip and ended up at the villa. He must have been waiting for her in her room—though how he knew she was here, God knows. But that's beside the point. She has been strangled. Her neck and throat are badly bruised. She needs a doctor at once.'

Quickly grasping the situation Mrs Lessing's anger towards Alex subsided: she could see by Cicely's swollen and discoloured neck that what he said was true. She left the room for a minute and then returned, saying, 'I have sent one of the servants for Dr Ott, and told them not to come back without him.'

'He's a good man?' demanded Alex.

'The best. Doctor Ott attends the king,' said Mrs Lessing.

Alex nodded. 'Good.'

'Gracious, Cicely,' said Sophie's voice from the doorway. The commotion had reached her bedroom and she had come downstairs to see what was going on. 'What happened to you?'

Cicely tried to speak again, but her throat was too sore and she sank back on to the sofa, exhausted.

'Not another word,' said her aunt. 'Sophie, you sit with Cicely. I will go and speak to the servants—they are beginning to wonder what is going on. And you,' she said to Alex, 'had better go with those detectives of yours and make sure they don't let Goss escape again.'

'I'm not going anywhere until I know Cicely's going to be all right,' he growled.

'If you think I am going to let you remain in the room whilst the doctor examines my niece you are very much mistaken,' she said with asperity.

'I will be . . . all right.' Cicely's words came out as a croak, but they were comprehensible. She put her hand on Alex's arm reassuringly.

Reluctantly he rose from her side. Realizing that she would be well looked after by her aunt and cousin, and knowing he could do no more to help her at present, Alex gave a curt nod. There was something in what Mrs Lessing said. He would be wise to make sure that the detectives did their job properly this time. After what had just occurred, he would not rest easily until Goss was under lock and key.

'Very well. But I will return first thing in the morning,' he said.

With a last look at Cicely, as if to reassure himself that she would indeed be all right, he departed, and Cicely gave herself over to the ministrations of her cousin and her aunt.

'What a shocking to-do,' said Mrs Lessing. 'Imagine that odious man escaping and attacking you—here in the villa, of all places. I would very much like to know how it came about.' She waved her hand as Cicely tried to speak. 'No, not now. It can wait until you are well again, my dear.'

CHAPTER TEN

'How are you feeling?'

It was the following morning and Sophie, eager to find out how Cicely was, had brought her breakfast in bed.

'Much better, thank you,' said Cicely.

Her ordeal of the night before now seemed like a dream, and if not for her painful throat she would have thought it had been simply that. But the livid marks round her neck bore witness to the fact that it had been real.

'Mr Evington has been here asking after you,' said Sophie, as she poured Cicely a cup of coffee. 'Mother told him you were asleep and that you could not be disturbed.'

Cicely's heart sank. Though her aunt's actions had been well intentioned, she would have liked to see Alex. There had been such a look of concern on his face the night before that she had wondered . . . had hoped . . . but of course, it was nothing but idle fancy.

'She told him the same the next time he called as well,' said Sophie, handing Cicely the coffee.

'He has been twice?' asked Cicely.

'Three times. You've slept late,' she explained, seeing Cicely's expression. 'He won't be calling again, though.'

Cicely felt her hand beginning to tremble, and put the cup down with a clatter.

'Is it too hot? I thought it might be. Let me put some more milk in for you.'

Cicely allowed Sophie to make the coffee cooler, although that had not been the reason for her almost dropping the cup.

'He won't be calling again, did you say?' asked Cicely with studied nonchalance.

'He has had to go back to England. But I dare say you will see him there when you return.'

'Yes. I dare say.'

So it was over then. Any thoughts she might have had about Alex's concern for her had been laid to rest, and now she had nothing to do but to go back to England and pretend that she was indifferent to him.

Yes. That was all.

266

'But you won't be well enough to travel for a while. I know Mother wants to keep you with us for as long as possible. And so do I.'

The thought gave Cicely some comfort. If she lingered in Marienbad, she might miss Alex altogether. With any luck, he would have returned to London before she went back home, and she would be spared the pain of seeing him again, and even worse, perhaps hearing about his plans to marry Miss Postlethwaite.

*　　　*　　　*

Cicely's sojourn in Austria lasted another week, but then she felt she could impose on her aunt and cousin no longer. Sophie and Mrs Lessing had a long-standing arrangement to visit Paris, and although they pressed her to join them she declined, saying it was time for her to return to the Lodge.

Her return journey was more sombre than her outward journey had been, and she was glad to reach England. So much had happened since she had gone away, and she was looking forward to the peace and quiet of home.

'It is good to have you back, miss,' said Gibson, as he welcomed her at the door. 'I trust you had an enjoyable time?'

Gibson had known nothing of Cicely's real reason for going to Marienbad, and had accepted at face value her story of going to pay a visit to her aunt, so she remarked simply, 'Yes, thank you, Gibson. It was most . . . satisfactory.'

Gibson departed, and Cicely strolled round the sitting-room, reacquainting herself with it, before going out into the garden. It looked much the same as it had looked when she had left. It was hard to believe that she had only been gone for such a short space of time. So much had happened.

She went back into the house and regarded herself in the mirror. She was fortunate that high necks were fashionable, as her lace-trimmed blouse covered up the remains of her bruises, and she would not have to explain them to her friends.

She took off her gloves and hat and then set about cutting some fresh flowers for the house. She had just finished when Alice bounded into the house.

'You're back.' Alice hugged her impulsively. 'Thank goodness. It's been so boring whilst you've been away.'

Not even Alice had known the truth behind Cicely's visit to Marienbad—the fewer people who had known of her plan, the less likelihood it had had of leaking out and alarming Martin Goss, putting him on his guard. But now that he was safely in custody, the time had come to reveal the truth.

'My time has been anything but boring . . .' she said.

'Well!' exclaimed Alice, when Cicely had finished her account of recent events. She shook her head. 'Well, I never. And so Martin Goss was the thief all along. Gladys will be delighted. And so will everyone else. It was an upsetting incident, but everyone will soon know the truth. You have only to tell Mrs Sealyham, and it will be all round Little Oakleigh, Oakleigh and Greater Oakleigh by this time tomorrow! And Mr Evington was in on it, too, you say? Only think, we all believed he had gone to London. Oh, Cicely, it's so good to have you back—both of you. Although I'm surprised he got here before you.'

Cicely's spirits sank. It was evident that Alex was still at the Manor.

'What is it?' asked Alice. 'Is it something about Mr Evington?'

Cicely could not tell Alice what was really troubling her, so instead she said, 'He will not be staying at the Manor for long. He only bought it so that he would be able to trap Martin Goss, and now that he no longer has any need for it he will be moving back to London.'

'Oh, Cicely, no.' Alice was dismayed. 'Does that mean he will be selling it again?'

Cicely nodded. She had not actually heard him say so, but if he had no further need for it, then she could not imagine he would want to keep it.

And just when I was getting used to having

269

him here,' said Alice.

Cicely turned away. She did not want Alice to see her face, for she was afraid her feelings were written there for all to see.

'Oh, well, never mind,' said Alice. 'Perhaps he will sell it to a family. People who will love it as a home. That is what you always wanted.'

Cicely did not trust herself to speak.

Alice, mistaking her silence, said, 'You must be tired after your long journey. I will leave you to unpack.' She got up and went over to the door. 'Oh. I almost forgot. Mother says you are invited to dinner tomorrow. Do say you'll come.'

Cicely was once more in command of herself. 'I'd love to. Thank you.'

Alice departed.

Cicely, walking over to the window, looked out over her small garden to the sweeping lawns beyond, and, in the distance, the Manor. Alex had evidently returned to sort out his affairs, but after that . . . ?

It did not bear thinking about. Because after that, he would sell the Manor and she would never see him again.

*　　　*　　　*

Just three more mornings to go, thought Cicely as she walked briskly up the drive on the following Monday, ready to discharge her duties as Alex's secretary. She had bumped into Roddy on returning home, and it had become evident that she was expected at the Manor on Monday, Wednesday and Friday mornings, after which Alex would be returning to London.

A part of her was devastated at the knowledge, and yet a part of her was relieved. Given that he did not return her feelings she would rather not have to see him again. She knew how difficult it was going to be for her to sit at the other side of the fine mahogany desk and help him with all the business relating to the Manor whilst all the time knowing that in a very short time he would be leaving, never to return. But still, she had taken on the job as his secretary and she meant to see it through.

As she approached the Manor, the front door opened and Roddy came out. On seeing Cicely he made straight for her.

'I still can't get over what a wonderful job you did in Marienbad,' he said enthusiastically, gripping her by the hand and shaking it.

If Alex had shaken her hand, her body would be on fire, thought Cicely, but with Roddy the gesture had no effect and was nothing more than a friendly salute.

'It is a relief we finally caught him,' Cicely replied.

'He will be behind bars for a very long time. But that isn't what I wanted to say to you. Alex asked me to tell you that he will not be able to see you this morning, or on Wednesday, after all, but hopes to see you for one last time on Friday.'

Cicely tried to hide her feeling of devastation at Roddy's words. She had not been looking forward to seeing Alex again. Indeed, she had been dreading it. But only now did she realize how much worse not seeing him would be.

'I . . .' She tried to make a suitable rejoinder, but her mind had frozen. The thought of having only one more meeting with Alex was truly awful.

'It's a dratted nuisance, and I know he's sorry to have inconvenienced you,' went on Roddy blithely.

Inconvenienced, thought Cicely with a feeling of utter desolation. If only Roddy knew. But she was thankful he did not.

She took a deep breath, and called on her pride to sustain her. Forcing her mouth into a smile she said, 'It is all right. I quite understand. He must have a lot to do.'

'Oh, Lord! Is that the time? I have to be going,' said Roddy, glancing at the watch that was slung across the front of his waistcoat. 'I'm going to see a man about a motor. I'm getting one of my own at last.'

He gave her a happy smile, and Cicely forced her own to remain until he was out of sight. Then she allowed it to sag. She felt exhausted, as though she had just run a race. But she must walk back to the Lodge.

As she stood there gathering her strength, she thought of the Manor being sold once more. Who would come to live there? Would it be a family? Or another cit? And what would become of it? Would the trees be cut down, or the library turned into a billiard room? She could not bear to think of it. And her father's collection. Would the new owner allow the velocipedes to remain in the stables, or would he clear them out, regarding them as nothing but old junk?

As she thought about her father's collection, her footsteps unconsciously took her towards the barn: she could not resist one last look. She opened the door, suppressing all thoughts of what had happened there only a few short weeks before, and ran her eyes lovingly over the velocipedes. Her father had given most of his life to the collection: it was dreadful to think of it being disposed of. But if it must be, it must be. Reconciling herself to the fact she closed the barn door and turned . . . to almost bump into Alex.

'Alex!' she exclaimed.

'Cicely!' he said, equally surprised.

He stood looking at her, and seemed as though he was about to speak. But then the light died in his eyes and he turned away.

She could not believe he was leaving. How could he go?

He hesitated. Then stopped.

Cicely's heart was in her mouth.

He turned, and the light fell full on the side of his face, giving his skin a wonderful sheen. She longed to reach out and touch it. She wanted to sink into his arms and feel his mouth on her own.

For a moment he looked as though he was going to claim her. His eyes were burning with a passionate intensity and his body was as taut as a bowstring. But then the fire died in his eyes. His body lost some of its tension. And he spoke.

'I am glad I have seen you. I was going to give you these on Friday, but I have decided not to stay. I will be returning to London this afternoon. And so I will give them to you now.'

He held out his hand, palm up, and she saw that something was lying there. And then she realized what it was.

'The keys?' She looked at him in perplexity, trying to read the answer to the puzzle in his face.

'Yes. The keys. I want you to have the Manor.'

'No. I couldn't.' For some reason the thought of living at the Manor again, of being there without Alex, was devastating. She put her hands behind her back. She didn't want the Manor. She knew it with every bone in her body. She wanted him.

'You helped me capture Martin Goss. I couldn't have done it without you. I will always be grateful to you.'

Grateful? What use was gratitude, she thought as he walked towards her.

Taking her arm, he pulled it gently from behind her back and opened her hand. He was so close she could smell his cologne. He had shaved recently, but already there was a hint of stubble on his chin. She wanted to touch it, feel it, run her hands over it. But she could not do it. If she did so it would awaken all her feelings for him, and they must be denied.

She stood like a statue, unfeeling, unmoving, as he put the keys in her hand and closed her fingers round them. As he did it his eyes never once left hers.

'I don't want a stranger living here,' he said. 'The Manor is yours.'

Then, with what seemed like an immense effort of will he turned and walked away.

'You won't leave without saying goodbye?' She should not have called after him, but she could not help herself. The thought of never seeing him again was just too terrible.

He half turned. But only half. He hesitated. 'No. I will call in at the Lodge this afternoon when I pass.'

She managed a smile. But once Alex was gone all restraint faded and a look of utter despair took its place.

*   *   *

I should not have asked him to say goodbye,

thought Cicely that afternoon as she paced the sitting-room back at the Lodge. It will only make matters worse. I should have resisted the temptation.

But she had not, and worrying about it now would not help.

She set about dusting the furniture, and had nearly finished when Chuff Chuff walked in unannounced.

'What ho, Cicely!' he said.

He could not have come at a worse time. Still, Cicely set about making him welcome.

'Chuff Chuff, how lovely to see you. Would you like some tea?'

'Not for me, no, Cicely old thing. I just popped in to set a date.'

Cicely's heart sank. He did not still think she could be persuaded to marry him? But one glance at his face told her this was so.

'Sit down, Chuff Chuff,' she said. She knew she had to explain to him, again, that she would never marry him, and this time she had to make sure he listened.

'Right-oh,' he said amiably.

'Chuff Chuff, I can never marry you,' she said, in what she hoped was an authoritative voice.

'It's no good, you living on your own,' said Chuff Chuff. 'Not even now Evington's given you the Manor.'

'What?' Cicely was dumbfounded. 'How did you know about that?'

'Cyril, the gardener. Saw him giving you the keys.'

Cicely's heart sank. In that case, the news would be all round Little Oakleigh by now.

'You still can't live there, Cicely old thing. You haven't got the money to do it. You shouldn't have to be living hand to mouth. Come to Parmiston. Or if you want to live at Oakleigh Manor we'll move in there. The mater told me to tell you that. Told me to tell you we'll use the Chuffington fortune. Do the place up a bit. Houseful of servants. Dinner parties. Houseparties. That kind of thing. House in London. Theatres. Plays. Go—'

'No.' Cicely's voice was firm. 'I can never marry you, Chuff Chuff, for the simple reason that I don't love you. I know your mother told you to ask me three times, and you've done it, but I won't change my mind. You're a dear, sweet man Chuff Chuff, and I love you as though you were my brother, but I can never marry you. I do beg you to believe me, for I don't want to have this conversation again.'

Chuff Chuff's face fell.

Cicely put a hand on his arm. 'There are plenty of other girls who would love to marry you.'

'Really?' he asked, his spirits rising.

'Really,' said Cicely firmly. 'I know for a fact that Gillian Fraser thinks you a very handsome man.'

'Gillian Fraser?' asked Chuff Chuff. Gillian

277

was a diffident young lady who lived in Nether Oakleigh.

Cicely nodded, and Chuff Chuff brightened.

'Oh, well. Not the same, of course,' he said, shaking his head. 'The Frasers aren't the Haringays. Still, the mater would be pleased,' he went on thoughtfully.

Cicely breathed a sigh of relief. She knew Chuff Chuff was disappointed, but she suspected that his marrying her had been his mother's idea rather than his own, and that Gillian would make him a more suitable match.

'Well, mustn't keep you,' he said, standing up. 'Better go talk it over with the mater. Toodle pip.' And with that he ambled out of the room. Cicely sank down into a chair. Only to spring out of it a minute later as she heard Chuff Chuff, from the hall, saying, 'What ho! Evington. Didn't see you standing there.'

Alex? He was here? But of course. He had come to say goodbye.

She had just time to smooth the wrinkles out of her skirt before he walked in the room. He stood there, framed in the doorway, a strange expression—a mixture of hope and fear—on his face.

'You refused Chuffington?' he asked.

There was such a look in his eyes that her mouth went dry and she quivered from head to foot. She tried to speak but no sound came out. She gave a slight nod.

'I thought you were going to marry him.'

'You had little faith in me,' she said, her voice returning as she remembered how quick he had been to believe she would marry Chuff Chuff so that she could live at Parmiston Manor.

'He told me you were betrothed.'

Cicely's eyes opened wide.

'At the ball,' he went on. 'After the theft of the necklace.'

'So that was why your manner changed,' she said, beginning to understand. She remembered the moment clearly. They had seemed so close, and then, suddenly, so far apart. 'But still, you believed him.'

'I had no reason to doubt him. And I did not know you then as I know you now. Marry me, Cicely.'

Her heart stopped beating. 'Marry you?' she asked, hardly daring to believe her ears.

'Yes, Cicely,' he said gently. 'Marry me.'

It could not be. She had thought he was leaving, but now here he was asking her to marry him. A surge of joy welled up inside her. But still, she had to know the truth of his feelings before she could answer him.

'If you hadn't overheard, would you really have left?' she asked.

'No.'

He took her hands, and sparks flared between them.

'I meant to go right away, and forget, or at

279

least, try to forget all about you. A spell on the Riviera, I thought, or a trip to the States. But I knew I couldn't do it. Not without coming here; saying you couldn't marry him; telling you you were not in love with him, that you were in love with me.'

'I know,' she sighed.

'You know?'

She nodded. 'I've known for a long time.' She took a step back. It took all of her courage and all of her strength but still she did it. She could not fall into his arms as she longed to do until she knew what his feelings were for her. 'But I still don't know how you feel about me.'

'Don't you? I'm in love with you, Cicely. I believe it started on the day I first saw you. You looked so appealing when you rode away from me on your bicycle that I couldn't help being stirred by you, but it was only when I came to know you that I realized how deep those stirrings were: not just the stirrings of my body but of my soul. And by the time of the Manor ball I knew that what I felt was love.'

'You knew it so soon?' asked Cicely in delight.

He nodded. Taking her arm he led her out into the garden.

'I had been denying it until then, telling myself that what I felt for you was respect, friendship, admiration, concern—anything but love. But the night of the ball changed everything. When I saw how upset you were at the idea of the tree being cut down—when I realized the Manor was not just a house to you but a home, as the tenement I grew up in, for all its faults, was mine—my heart ached for you. God, how it ached! I wanted to fold you in my arms and promise you that I would never let anything change. My heart was already yours by then but I would not admit it. It was not until I saw you with Gladys that the last of my defences were stripped away.' He saw her puzzled look and explained, 'I had been denying my feelings for you by reminding myself that you came from the landed gentry, a class of people who had wrongly accused my sister of theft and turned her off without a reference; a class of people I despised. But when I heard you talking to Gladys I realized that I couldn't have been more wrong in thinking you were the same. You not only comforted her, you were determined to make sure she didn't suffer by being wrongly accused. I could no longer hide from my feelings by telling myself that you would have turned against my sister. I knew it to be false. If you had been there you would have comforted her, and found her another post. And with the last of my defences stripped away I had to admit the truth: that I was in love with you.' He paused. And then Chuffington told me that you and he were engaged. In the space of a few seconds I went from a glimpse of Heaven to the depths of Hell.'

'So that is why you were so distant when I told you of my plan to trap Goss.'

He nodded. 'I was angry with you for having agreed to marry a man you didn't love, and angry with myself for having allowed myself to fall in love with you. And so I made up my mind to forget about you. But then you came up with a plan for trapping Goss and I couldn't resist, even though it would mean being with you. Something I felt unequal to.'

'As I felt unequal to being with you,' Cicely admitted. 'Every time I saw you I wanted—' She broke off, confused.

'Yes?' He turned to face her.

'I wanted you to take me in your arms and kiss me.'

'Like this?' he asked, suiting the action to the words.

'Yes,' she gasped as he finally let her go. 'Like that. But then you accused me of being about to marry so that I could live at Parmiston Manor.'

'I should never have doubted you.'

'If Chuff Chuff told you we were betrothed, you had no choice,' she sighed.

'Yes, I did. I should have asked you if it was true. I tried to do it, but I could not bring myself to say the words. Because I could not bear to hear the answer.'

'I understand.' She hesitated, and then said, 'You seemed very fond of Miss Postlethwaite.'

'Eugenie?' he asked in surprise. 'Yes. I am.'

'Oh,' she said in a small voice.

He turned her to look at him. 'Can it be that you are jealous?'

She raised her eyes to his. 'Now that I know you love me I am jealous of no one.'

He laughed. 'It's a good thing. Because Miss Postlethwaite is not Miss Postlethwaite at all. She is Mrs Dortmeyer.'

Cicely looked startled.

'Eugenie lived next door to us when we were children. She set out to seek her fate, and found it in the form of Hyram Dortmeyer. She married him, and they have lived happily together ever since.'

Cicely laughed. 'And to think, when I saw you fastening the necklace round her neck . . .' She stopped, realizing she had given too much away.

'You thought Eugenie and I . . . ?' he asked, in astonishment. Then burst out laughing. 'Eugenie is a fine woman, but I would never want to take her in my arms like this'—he embraced her—'or kiss her like this'—his lips found her own . . . and for a long time nothing more was said. 'Or offer her my hand,' he said, suddenly serious. 'You still haven't answered me, Cicely.' He looked directly into her eyes. 'Will you marry me?'

She answered simply, 'Yes.'

He kissed her again. 'We will live at the Manor, and not a thing will be changed.'

Cicely smiled. 'There are some things I

would like to change,' she said.

'Name them, and it will be done.'

He led her back inside, and together they talked over the plans for the Manor. The Manor had brought them together, and it was only fitting it should be their new home once they were married.

'And when it is done, we can hold our wedding breakfast there,' said Alex with satisfaction. 'The first celebration we hold there together will be to celebrate our marriage.'

'Marriage?' The voice took them by surprise. Alice was just entering through the french doors, grinning from ear to ear. 'Oh, Cicely, I'm so happy for you. Say I can be a bridesmaid.'

'Of course,' laughed Cicely. 'I wouldn't have it any other way.'

EPILOGUE

The day of the wedding dawned bright and fair. Cicely felt a mixture of nerves and excitement as Sophie helped her to arrange her veil over her face. The veil was a beautiful confection made of the finest lace. It complemented the beauty of her gown to perfection. Made by Maison Worth, the high-necked gown was a most exquisite creation. Its silk bodice was inset with rows of ruffled lace, and its long train was decorated with lace flounces. The bodice was tight, with a tiered skirt opening at the front to reveal a ruched underskirt, matched by lace-trimmed sleeves. As a finishing touch, she wore white gloves and the most delectable silk slippers.

'You look beautiful,' Sophie breathed.

Sophie and her mother had come over to Little Oakleigh for the occasion, and they were not the only two visitors. Alex's sister, Katie, had also arrived. Like Sophie, she was one of Cicely's bridesmaids and the two girls were wearing beautiful silk-and-lace gowns that complemented Cicely's own.

The third bridesmaid, Alice, was at that moment nowhere to be seen.

'I hope Alice is here soon,' said Cicely anxiously, as her nerves momentarily got the better of her. 'In another few minutes we will have to leave for the church. What is she doing?'

Sophie chuckled, but would say no more than, 'There is something she has to do. But don't worry, she'll be here on time.'

Sure enough, at that moment Alice arrived. She was grinning from ear to ear, but Cicely was too nervous and excited to ask her what she had been doing. Instead she took a deep breath and, picking up her bouquet, led the way downstairs.

One by one they took their places in Alex's Daimlers, two being needed for the short drive to the church.

And then they were there.

Cicely stepped out of the Daimler. Gibson, stepping out of the car beside her, almost burst with pride. His delight at being asked to give Cicely away was plain to see. He held himself erect, head up, back straight.

Cicely stood patiently whilst Alice arranged her train, then took Gibson's arm and walked through the lych gate and up the path to the church.

It was full to overflowing. Everyone in Little Oakleigh had turned out to see Cicely's marriage. They were all delighted that she was to marry the owner of the Manor, and even more delighted that she was to marry Alex, who had become an inalienable part of the village. And there, her leg newly mended, was Cousin Gertrude, who had arrived to be

Cicely's chaperon just as a chaperon was no longer needed.

From within came the strains of the organ, growing louder as Cicely approached the church door.

She took a deep breath, and then stepped into the church.

As she began to process down the aisle on Gibson's arm, every head turned. But Cicely did not see her friends. Mrs Murgatroyd's smiles and Lady Chuffington's sniffs passed her by. She only had eyes for Alex.

He was waiting for her at the altar. His immaculate suit showed off his splendid physique, and as she saw the look of love in his eyes she was filled with joy at knowing that she was going to be his wife.

*   *   *

The bells pealed cheerfully as Cicely and Alex left the church. A crowd of well-wishers had gathered outside, and the two newly-weds were showered with rice in a traditional gesture of goodwill. As they ran through the shower to the waiting Daimler, something caught Alex's eye. Bending down he scooped up a handful of rice. In and amongst the creamy grains were a number of shapes, cut out of pink paper. He held them on his open palm and looked enquiringly at Cicely.

Cicely, seeing what he held, began to smile,

and then began to laugh.

'What . . . ?' he asked in surprise.

'So that's what Alice was doing!' said Cicely. She turned to Alex. 'When you first arrived in Little Oakleigh, Alice said how wonderful it would be if I were to marry you. And I said—'

'Don't tell me. Let me guess!' He looked at his palm again, smiling at the sight of the little pink pigs, each with their own set of wings. He threw them into the air, and as they swirled and danced in the air currents he said, 'Pigs will fly!'

They went out of the lych gate and stepped into the Daimler, then together they drove back to the Manor.

We hope you have enjoyed this Large Print book. Other Chivers Press or Thorndike Press Large Print books are available at your library or directly from the publishers.

For more information about current and forthcoming titles, please call or write, without obligation, to:

Chivers Press Limited
Windsor Bridge Road
Bath BA2 3AX
England
Tel. (01225) 335336

OR

Thorndike Press
295 Kennedy Memorial Drive
Waterville
Maine 04901
USA

All our Large Print titles are designed for easy reading, and all our books are made to last.